Rebel Wolf

Book 4
Aloha Shifters: Pearls of Desire

by Anna Lowe

Twin Moon Press

Editing by Lisa A. Hollett

Covert art by Kim Killion

ISBN: 9781720213949

Contents

Other books in this series

Aloha Shifters - Pearls of Desire

Rebel Dragon (Book 1)

Rebel Bear (Book 2)

Rebel Lion (Book 3)

Rebel Wolf (Book 4)

Rebel Alpha (Book 5)

visit www.annalowebooks.com

Free Books

Get your free e-books now!

Sign up for my newsletter at *annalowebooks.com* to get three free books!

- *Desert Wolf*: Friend or Foe (Book 1.1 in the Twin Moon Ranch series)

- *Off the Charts* (the prequel to the Serendipity Adventure series)

- *Perfection* (the prequel to the Blue Moon Saloon series)

Chapter One

"So, you and Sophie have a date, huh?" Dell asked.

Chase drove down the coastal highway, sticking to the speed limit of forty-five, ignoring Dell and his shit-eating grin.

Yes, he and Sophie had a date, and he was counting down the hours, minutes, and seconds. The thing was, it would be easier to shift into wolf form and show the way he felt than to put it into words. He'd wag his tail furiously, then turn a couple of circles in sheer glee. After that, he'd roll over a few times and bounce around like a drunken kangaroo.

But he was in human form, and that complicated things. Humans liked talking. Which was weird, because they didn't always mean what they said. Of course, Dell was a friend and a fellow shifter. But Dell had the gift of gab, while Chase, well. . . not so much.

Mate, his wolf side murmured, daydreaming again.

"Yep," he murmured absently.

Chase grinned as he drove. He loved Sophie's honest smile and the way it always brightened when she spotted him. Her thick chestnut hair, braided in a different style each day. Her wary doe eyes that seemed to shine and sparkle just for him. Deep, forest-green eyes that reminded him of the woods back home.

He heaved a love-sick sigh, checked the clock on the dashboard, and updated his countdown once more. Eight hours, thirty-two minutes, and fifty seconds until the most important moment of his life.

"What are you guys planning to do?" Dell asked.

Chase scratched his ear — one of the simple pleasures of being in human form, because he didn't have to sit on his ass

1

and try to reach it with his rear paw. Then he shrugged. The details of his date didn't matter as long as he got to be with Sophie. She'd said something about going for a walk. Or was it a drive to Nakalele Blowhole? Either way, it was bound to be great.

Except for the fact that ever since that morning, he'd been shadowed by a feeling of foreboding. The feeling of danger creeping in. He sniffed the air. Was that the real thing or a false alarm? Having grown up entirely among wolves, he was often confused by the human world. And ever since he and his brothers had retired from Special Forces and settled down on Maui, they'd struggled to balance a sense of peace with the need to remain vigilant. The world was full of ruthless enemies who could strike anywhere, anytime.

Was today one of those days? Chase sniffed the salt air, trying to decide.

"Are you taking Sophie to lunch?" Dell asked. "Oh, I know. You can bring her to the Lucky Devil." The lion shifter cackled at his own joke.

"No way," Chase growled. He might not know much about the human world, but he knew not to bring the woman he loved to his workplace on their first date.

Eight hours, thirty-one minutes... his wolf murmured.

"I brought Anjali there before we got together." Dell flashed one of those *I'm so in love* grins. "Oh, oh. Did I tell you what Quinn — best baby in the world — did this morning? It was the cutest thing. We're waking up, Anjali and me, and Quinn was lying on my chest..."

Normally, Chase wouldn't have tuned out, but his mind kept drifting back to Sophie. From the moment they'd met, he'd known she was his destiny. One look, one sniff, and his fate was sealed.

Humans struggled to identify the person they were meant to spend forever with, and half the time, they got it wrong. But wolf shifters knew from the bottom of their hearts to the deepest reaches of their souls. They absolutely, positively *knew* in a way no human ever could.

The problem was, he'd met Sophie months ago, and he still hadn't figured out how to explain it all to her. Humans didn't understand about mates, and since he wasn't exactly a poet with words... Chase's brothers and Dell had been egging him on, encouraging him to take the next step with Sophie. The thing was, none of them realized how tenuous his hold on his human side was. Being around Sophie drove his wolf wild, and he was afraid he'd go too far, too fast.

"Then Quinn rolls over and says *ba-ba*. *Ba-ba* — isn't that cute? So I said *Ka-quinn* and she said *ba-ba* and Anjali said..."

Dell rambled through another of his *I love my mate and baby so much* stories. Not that Chase could blame the guy. Hell, if he had a mate and a child...

He cleared his throat and concentrated on the road. That dream would never come true if he didn't win over Sophie first. He couldn't win over Sophie if he didn't impress her on their date. And he'd never impress her if he stayed this jittery. Damn it, what was making him feel so off-balance?

He sniffed the air again, then interrupted Dell with a curt, "You feel that?"

Dell looked around. "Feel what?"

"It's like something is wrong. Something out of place."

Dell sniffed around then shook his head. "Life couldn't be better, man. You're just nervous about your date. Don't worry. It'll be great."

Chase *was* nervous, but that didn't account for the feeling of impending doom.

Dell smacked him on the shoulder. "Calm down, wolf."

Chase frowned. That was the crux of the matter. Most shifters were dominated by their human sides, but he'd grown up in the wild as the son of a full-blooded she-wolf. He hadn't joined his brothers in the human world until he was a teen. Even after all these years, it still overwhelmed him at times.

"Anyway, then Quinn did the most incredible thing," Dell went on. "She kissed me and said *Da-da*. Not *ba-ba* — *Da-da!* Isn't that amazing?"

"Amazing," Chase mumbled as he slowed the battered pickup, getting ready to park on the outskirts of town.

3

As far as human settlements went, Lahaina was pretty nice. Not too big, not too loud. It got crowded with tourists at times, but mostly people were relaxed and friendly. Not like some places he'd been.

The best thing about Lahaina, though, was the fact that he'd met Sophie there, and that he could count on seeing her nearly every day. She ran the smoothie truck in a seaside park, and when he had walked by one day, months ago. . .

His chest heated as he relived the moment. It had been as if gravity had suddenly tripled, because he could barely move except to turn his head. Even before he spotted Sophie, he'd fallen in love, just from the vibes she gave off. She was a ray of sunshine breaking through the clouds, filling him with everything he yearned for. Hope. Interest. A newfound lust for life.

"Hey, quit daydreaming," Dell admonished when the car started to drift off the road. "I've got a mate and child to get home to, you know."

Chase snapped his attention back to the road. "Sorry."

Not sorry, his wolf griped. *Not for thinking about my mate.*

Within seconds, his thoughts wandered back to Sophie. It had gotten to the point that he felt more settled in town than at home, simply because Sophie was there. Not only did he get to see her, but he got to talk to her too. They'd even danced once, and his soul still soared when he thought back on that. He'd gotten to shut his eyes, hold her close, and sniff her heavenly scent. So maybe for their date, they ought to try dancing again.

Or walking, his inner wolf said. *Or howling to the moon. That would be nice.*

He sighed. Howling to the moon was out. But walking would be fine.

Except for that unsettled feeling that grew worse and worse.

They parked and started walking the ten blocks to their brunch shift at the Lucky Devil, the seaside restaurant where Chase ran security while Dell tended bar. Chase glanced left and right. On the face of it, everything looked normal in town. Shopkeepers emerged from the frontier-style buildings on either side of the road and set out colorful signs. A Hawaiian flag fluttered from a rooftop in wavy red, white, and blue stripes. The streets were wet and tidy, having just been sprayed down and cleaned. The usual morning routine, in other words.

"What's the rush, man?" Dell asked.

Chase frowned. His walk was a near jog, and he couldn't say why. Only that instinct told him to get moving — and fast.

Dell laughed, continuing his easy stroll while Chase rushed ahead. "Oh, right. You want to get a smoothie before work. A smoothie and a look at your girl. I know how it is, man."

Chase broke into a jog, leaving Dell behind. How could Dell know how it felt? Ever since Dell had met Anjali, he'd gotten to spend hours with his destined mate. He got to start and finish every day by gazing into her eyes. Chase only got to spend a little time with Sophie once or twice a day. Seeing Sophie was heaven, but saying goodbye was hell. The only reason he'd been able to hold out for so long was the fact that he could sense her nearby while he was at work.

He reached out with his mind, feeling for that bright, sunny spot that was Sophie. He couldn't actually see her, and he couldn't read her mind, but he could sense her, and that always felt good.

He closed his eyes for a second, then frowned. All he could pick up on was the desperate barking of her dogs.

Bad. Bad. Bad, they bayed in alarm.

His step faltered before he caught himself and rushed ahead. What was going on?

"Hey, man. Where's the fire?" Dell called from behind.

Chase jolted from a run into an all-out sprint. The lush leaves of the town park fluttered like any other day, but the closer he got, the more he could feel the dogs' panic.

Bad. Bad. Get away.

Chase hit his top gear and hurtled around the corner, then screeched to a stop. There was Sophie, over by a tree where the dogs were tied. There was the smoothie truck where she worked, a few steps away. All perfectly normal, right?

Then, *BOOM!* An explosion ripped through the air, and Sophie was thrown back. His Sophie, flung like a rag doll. An echo of a scene he'd seen far too many times in war zones, but one he'd never, ever imagined occurring in Maui.

"Sophie!" he yelled, rushing in.

Chapter Two

Sophie had started her morning shift at work by frowning at her phone. Of all the people to have received an out-of-the-blue message from, David Orren was the last person she expected — or wanted — to get in touch with.

Heya, Sophie. I'm visiting Maui. We really need to get together. So much to catch up on. All the good times.

She scowled. If their childhood had been such a good time, why was she working so hard to forget it? Including David, the boy next door who'd always had a way of taking things too far.

Her hands clawed the air in an echo of the time she'd had to escape his forced kiss. Then she punched her phone off, erasing his message. David might be interested in her, but she sure wasn't interested in him.

She straightened her shoulders and reminded herself to smile. It was going to be a great day on Maui, and nothing was going to ruin that. She had a date with Chase Hoving, the man she'd been crushing on for months, and all of Maui seemed to be celebrating with her. The sun was glittering off the ocean, the palms were swaying gently, and the morning breeze was clear and fresh.

So why were her dogs so alarmed?

"Coco. Darcy. Boris — shh!" She snapped her fingers.

Every day, she brought the dogs to Lahaina with her, and normally, they were perfectly happy to lounge in the shade of a nearby tree while she worked at the Sunshine Smoothies truck. On a good day, she'd blend up to two hundred fruit smoothies, so there was plenty of prep to do.

But the dogs kept snarling and straining at the end of their leashes, and she had no choice but to leave the truck to calm them down. No one had ever objected to her dogs being in the seaside park, but if they kept up that racket, she'd have trouble, for sure.

"Coco!" she admonished. "Boris! Darcy! Calm down."

But the dogs she'd rescued from a shelter didn't so much as glance in her direction. They were all fixated on something — or someone — near the rear of the smoothie truck.

"I told you. It's nothing," she muttered.

The trio had been barking for a good five minutes — about the time she'd heard a scratch on the outside of the truck. Even now, as she double-checked, she couldn't see anything out of the ordinary. A sanitation crew was moving through the park as they did every morning, emptying trash cans and raking up the huge leaves of the breadfruit trees.

She shook her finger at the dogs. "Enough already."

Coco wagged her tail meekly. Darcy stopped growling but continued to bare his teeth at the imaginary danger — but that was par for the course with Darcy, who saw everyone as an enemy. Boris barked once more then looked at Sophie for approval.

"Would you guys be quiet?"

She tried to be stern, but it was hard. Coco, a mangy little brown mutt, had been neglected in the past, and it showed in her desperate desire to please. Darcy, the Jack Russell, was a born fighter in spite of his diminutive size. Boris was a sleek, meek greyhound who rarely let out so much as a yelp. So what was riling him up now?

Sophie turned around and froze. What was that shadow moving behind the smoothie truck? A stab of fear went through her before she caught herself. Damn it, she was not going to be paranoid. The world wasn't the dark, danger-fraught place she'd been raised to fear. There was beauty and hope too. It was all a question of perspective. And she was determined to keep a positive outlook, no matter what it took.

"See? Everything is all right." She petted the dogs, slowly settling them down. Boris and Coco wound around each other, vying for the best position near Sophie's legs. Darcy, meanwhile, continued glaring into the distance with eyes that flashed with anger and hate.

"It's okay, guys," she said, smoothing down their bristling fur. "Now, listen. You have to be quiet, or I can't bring you to work."

Even Darcy sobered at that, and Coco stuck her tail between her legs. They might not have understood her words, but they couldn't miss the warning in her voice.

"So calm down. It's going to be a great day. A beautiful day. You want to know why?"

Coco wagged her tail and leaned closer.

"Well, first, we're on Maui, so that makes it great," Sophie explained. "Second, I have a date with Chase."

Her heart swelled at the thought. A date. A real date — with Chase! She'd been pining after the calm, quiet man with dark, mysterious eyes for weeks.

Coco tilted her head, and her ears flopped as if to say, *Weeks?*

Sophie sighed. Okay, so it had been more like months. She'd been trying to work up the nerve to ask Chase out, but as it turned out, he'd beaten her to it.

Sophie, would you like to go out with me? he'd asked, shifting from foot to foot and looking a little flushed. His hands had been shoved deep into his pockets, and he'd bitten his lip in hope.

The man could go from *muscled warrior* to *shy and innocent* in the blink of an eye, and neither persona was for show.

That would be very nice, she'd managed to say in the wave of euphoria that made her cheeks burn and her heart thump.

She hugged Boris, reliving the joy of that moment. Chase wanted to go on a date — with her!

So, yes. It was going to be a great day. Maybe the best of her life. Because honestly, she wasn't just crushing on Chase. She was head over heels in love and had been from day one. The very first time she'd seen Chase, she'd gone warm all over. His hazel eyes had locked on hers, and he'd stopped in his tracks to stare at her from across the park. She'd stared back while her heart hammered and her breath grew short. Someone might as well have lined up dozens of magnets and caught the two of them in their powerful field. So, wow. Maybe there really was such a thing as love at first sight.

In her head, Sophie could imagine a dozen different ways to start a sparkling conversation with Chase. But sadly, she wasn't like the heroines of her favorite books, who always found something clever to say. In real life, her mouth would go dry, her tongue would twist, and she couldn't so much as peep. As it turned out, Chase wasn't the slick talker some of her book boyfriends were either. In fact, he barely uttered a word, though his eyes had lit up and shone as he took her in. A damn good thing for her job at the smoothie truck...

Hi, he'd said, coming up that first day.

In truth, he'd been shoved in her direction by Dell, but every step after the first was of his own free will. Quick, eager steps that said more than his words.

Hi, she'd replied, grateful for the counter that hid how much her knees were shaking.

They had just stood there for a while, gazing into each other's eyes. Falling deeply, desperately, hopelessly in love.

Hi might have been as far as they'd ever gotten if it hadn't been for Chase's friend Dell, who'd stepped up beside him and ordered a smoothie. All relaxed and casual, as if it had been any other day and not the most amazing moment in Sophie's life.

I'd like a tropical swirl, please. What do you want, Chase?

Which was how she'd learned Chase's name. Lord knew she never would have had the nerve to ask him. Even then, it took her another three weeks to work up the nerve to say, *Hi, Chase.*

Two syllables instead of one. That was progress, right?

Chase had grinned from ear to ear and whispered back, *Hi, Sophie.*

So yes, they'd been taking things slowly, because she'd learned the hard way about the mistakes a girl might make. A mistake like David.

She shoved her phone — and the ugly memories — deeper into her pocket and concentrated on the good instead.

She'd been wary of Chase at first, as she was of all people. But the more she got to know him, the more she trusted her feelings. Just being around him made her happy, and every time he smiled, she felt like doing somersaults. He worked a few blocks away from the smoothie truck, which meant she got to see him nearly every day. And the days she didn't... well, she dreamed about him. A lot.

She might not be the bold, assertive type. But neither was Chase — except in the times she'd seen him and his friends in one of their darker moments. The dog tags around their necks spoke of a military background, and it showed in their watchful eyes and muscular physiques. Most of the time, they were fairly laid-back, but occasionally, something would put them on red alert. A raw, simmering *something* would hover around their shoulders, making passersby hurry aside.

But once whatever had set them off passed, they would go back to being the nice, normal guys everyone loved. Dell was the wildly popular bartender at the Lucky Devil. His Hollywood smile and leonine good looks were all part of the draw, and women practically swooned at the sight. Chase worked security at the front door, and he was just as handsome, but in a totally different way. His draw came from his quiet, unassuming manner and rugged good looks — not to mention that lean, chiseled body. He always looked like he'd just wandered back into civilization from a long, edge-of-survival expedition in the wilderness. His brown hair was slightly mussed, and his hazel eyes appeared startled at the hubbub all around. Sometimes, his speech was a little clunky and his manners painfully careful, like he was terrified of messing up.

"He's so sweet," most women said.

"Adorable," others would coo.

Like a modern-day Tarzan who was slowly adapting to civilization after years in the jungle, Sophie thought.

Thank goodness he didn't fall for the fluttery eyelids of women who tried to flirt their way into his bed. Chase didn't seem interested in anyone — except her.

Sophie's cheeks flushed. Kind, polite, sweet Chase liked her — plain old her! — and she had a date with him that very afternoon.

"I have to get back to work," she murmured to the dogs. Then she straightened and tipped her head back, drinking in the sunlight while rubbing the heart-shaped locket she always wore around her neck. Life could be beautiful, and she was the luckiest woman on earth. She stepped toward the smoothie truck, smiling.

But the hair on the back of her neck stood in alarm, and a deep, dark voice whispered in her mind.

Stop. Don't.

Don't what? she wanted to ask. She paused, studying the truck. Sunlight glinted off the silver sides and shone in the curves of the propane cylinders at one end. Nothing looked wrong, but something certainly *felt* wrong.

"Don't be ridiculous," she muttered. She'd come to Maui to escape the constant fear and suspicion she'd grown up with. She was on a mission to banish all negatives from her head.

But Coco was whining, and Boris grabbed her pant leg to drag her back. Darcy stretched his muzzle forward and bared his teeth at an invisible foe.

"Silly dogs," Sophie sighed.

Well, she had been planning to say that. But halfway through *silly*, an explosion ripped through the air. The smoothie truck heaved, and thunder boomed in her ears. A heat wave rushed through the air, knocking her back. She flew backward then hit the ground hard. The dogs broke into hysterical barks as her world dimmed.

Woof woof woof woof, they went, making her head spin.

"Sophie? Sophie!" someone yelled.

But all she saw were stars, and all she felt was pain.

Chapter Three

A wave of heat buffeted Chase's body, and a slew of horrifying images flooded his mind. He'd witnessed plenty of explosions, and none of them was good. Not even the ones set off by the good guys.

But, shit. Those had all been in war zones. How the hell could it be happening here?

A woman screamed. Footsteps rushed over the ground. Every mynah bird in the nearby banyan tree took to the air, chattering in alarm.

"Sophie," he called, rushing forward.

Moving in awkward jerks, she climbed to her feet, but her knees buckled. He caught her arm and held her steady.

"Chase?" she whispered, gripping his arm.

His heart pounded halfway out of his chest. She was alive! He'd never seen her eyes go so wide or her hands shake so violently, but she was alive.

Sophie stumbled toward the flaming wreckage of the smoothie truck. "Oh God. The cash register. I should get the money."

He pulled her back. No way. If her favorite book had been in danger of burning, he'd go after it for her. A dog, no question. But money? Absolutely not.

One of the dogs was tucked into a terrified bundle, while Darcy raged on. Flames swirled around the truck, making evil, crackling sounds. From what Chase could tell, the smaller, reserve cylinder of propane had blown. The larger, primary cylinder was still there, engulfed in flames.

"Whoa," he murmured, pulling Sophie back.

"Wait," she protested.

A wall of heat reached out toward them like the hand of death. That second cylinder was going to blow, and when it did...

Take cover, a voice yelled inside his head. *Now!*

He spun and knocked Sophie to the ground, covering her body with his.

"Cha—" she started, but the second explosion drowned her out.

It flattened Chase, and he closed his eyes, telling himself the pain didn't matter. Not the hot trickle of blood in his ears, nor the awkward angle of his arms as he covered as much of Sophie as he could. Little explosions flashed in his mind. Slowly, the pain ebbed away, and other than the sound of his own breath, there was nothing.

He blinked a couple of times and heaved a deep breath. Whoa. What had just happened?

"Chase," Sophie whispered. Or was she screaming? He couldn't tell. She was crying, for sure, and that gutted him. A slobbery tongue lapped at one side of his face, and he fended it off.

All in all, he ought to have been miserable, but with Sophie there cradling his head — well, it felt pretty good. Really good, in one way, even if his body didn't agree. She had her hair up in a braid that circled her head like a crown, and he longed to reach out and touch it.

"Are you okay?" Sophie asked, cupping his face.

He nearly smiled, because he was in heaven, or pretty close. He could have gazed into her eyes for eternity. But then again, those had been some hellish explosions, and he couldn't lie around waiting for blast number three.

Someone ran in with a fire extinguisher and started spraying wildly. In the distance, sirens wailed. If Chase could have covered his ears and crawled away, he would have. Supposedly, sirens were good because they meant help was on the way. He'd learned that the first season he'd come out of the wild to live with his half brothers. But sirens were right up there with flashing lights to a mind wired like a canine's, and Chase wanted to howl, like one of the dogs was doing just then.

He rolled over, got to his knees, then stood with Sophie's support. "I'm okay," he croaked. "What about the dogs?"

Sophie squeaked and ran over to hug the closest one. "Oh, Coco. Are you all right?"

Coco whimpered, though Chase couldn't see any sign of injury, and when he tuned in to the dog's thoughts, all he found was terror, not pain. The second Sophie hugged Coco, the little dog exhaled and calmed down.

Chase smiled faintly. Yeah, he knew that feeling, all right.

"My poor baby," Sophie cried, leaning over Boris, the newest of her growing pack.

The greyhound whimpered too, but mostly, he was eating up the attention. Darcy, on the other hand, snarled murderously in the direction of the truck.

Wolf shifters could read dogs' minds to a certain degree. At least, whatever there was to read, which wasn't much once you took away the basics like *I'm hungry, I'm happy,* and *That bush is the best bush because I marked it with my pee.* Chase had an advantage, having a purebred wolf as a mother, which made it easier for him than most. Still, Coco and Boris were fairly useless at the moment. All he could get from them was fear mixed with the bliss set off by Sophie's attention. But Darcy was a tough little bastard — as tough as the most hardened soldiers Chase had met, and his mind was a little clearer.

Bad man. Bad man, Darcy barked and barked.

Chase kneeled and followed the dog's eyes, but all he saw were flames.

Come on, buddy. Tell me, he urged, petting Darcy.

Darcy bared his teeth and glanced up with a spiteful expression that said, *I'm only telling you because it will help my nice lady.*

Chase gave him a stern look, reminding Darcy he was top dog. In truth, though, he admired the Jack Russell's devotion to Sophie. Obviously, the little guy had suffered a lot of abuse in the past — or, as Chase was starting to think, he'd witnessed another *nice lady* be abused by some asshole of a husband. Whatever Darcy had experienced, it was enough to make him burn with anger and hate. But Sophie was Darcy's hero, his shining angel, and he'd do anything for her.

So tell me, Chase insisted. *You want to be a good dog, right?*

Being a good dog was the pinnacle of life's purpose as far as most canines were concerned, and Darcy gulped as if taking the world's most solemn oath. *Darcy is a good dog. Darcy loves the nice lady.*

So, help me help your nice lady. What did you see?

Darcy's eyes darkened, and a series of staccato images raced through his mind.

Bad man.

Chase saw a figure leaning over the propane cylinders while Sophie worked, ignorant of the danger she was in.

Mess.

The figure fumbled with something. A detonator? Chase couldn't tell, because Darcy's eyes only caught things a dog could understand.

Hurting my nice lady.

Flames swirled, and Darcy grumbled under his breath. If the little guy had been big enough, he would have covered Sophie with his body the way Chase had.

Chase was desperate for more information, but that was all he could get. He reached down to rub Darcy's ears, and it killed him when the dog winced and skittered away. Why couldn't the dog understand he didn't mean any harm? He sighed, giving Darcy some space, and settled for rewarding him with the ultimate praise.

"Good boy."

Darcy grumbled until Sophie came over and scratched his chin.

"My poor sweetie," she murmured.

Chase touched her back, assuring her Darcy was all right.

"Whoa. Are you two all right?" Dell asked, rushing up to Chase's side.

"Gas explosion. The cylinder just went," one bystander yelled to another as a fire truck pulled up. "Some kind of malfunction."

Dell glanced at Chase and shot a question directly into his mind. *Malfunction? What do you think?*

Chase started shaking his head, but that made his ears ring, so he stopped. That cylinder hadn't blown on its own. Someone had tampered with it or planted a detonator.

Dell's brow furrowed. *Who? Why?*

Chase scanned the growing crowd. That was what he wanted to know. But firemen were running around, gesturing for him, Sophie, and Dell to step back, and he still couldn't think straight.

"Wait. The dogs," Sophie protested, fumbling with their leashes. Dell helped, and before long, they were all huddled over by the seawall while the firemen sprayed foam over the inferno consuming the smoothie truck.

"Oh my God," Sophie breathed.

Chase didn't have to read her mind to know she was picturing what might have happened if she hadn't stepped out.

She turned toward him at exactly the same moment he turned to her, and within the space of a heartbeat, they were hugging. Chase rocked back and forth a little, fighting the sting in his eyes.

You okay? Dell asked, using the mental connection closely bonded shifters shared.

Chase squeezed his eyes shut. Yes, because Sophie was okay. No, because it had been close. What if he'd lost her?

He hung on without saying a word. The dogs clustered around their feet, forming a furry wall.

"Hey, guys," Dell murmured to the dogs. "Give them some space."

But the dogs didn't budge, and even a feline like Dell had to understand why. They were protecting the woman they loved. Ready to lay down their lives for Sophie if that's what it took.

Just like me, Chase murmured, holding her close. *Just like me.*

17

Chapter Four

Sophie's heart hammered, and her mind raced with terrifying thoughts. What if she'd been in the truck when the cylinder blew? What if the dogs had been hurt?

But the moment she fell into Chase's arms, all she felt was relief. She closed her eyes and buried her face in his shoulder, taking longer and deeper breaths. It was as if Chase was made for her, because everything fit just right. His shoulder was at exactly the right height, and her arms looped comfortably around his neck. His chest rose and fell in time with hers, and his arms kept her nice and snug against his warmth, totally safe. She inhaled, savoring his fresh, woodsy scent. The dogs huddled around her ankles, and the fire crackled in the background, but her mind stayed pleasantly blank.

"Uh, guys. . . " Dell murmured.

Chase didn't move, and Sophie didn't want to either. But the police rushed up, and she reluctantly pulled away.

"Miss. . . Miss. . . " a police officer called.

Chase stepped forward, blocking the way. The dogs did the same, baring their teeth, and Sophie's heart warmed. For so long, she'd been alone. A nobody with no one to care whether she existed or not. Now, she was surrounded by love. A solid wall of it, showing her just how special she was.

The police officer stepped back, looking nowhere near as confident as he had a moment before. "Take it easy, everyone. I need you to move to a safe distance, miss. Then I need you to call off your dogs." His eyes dropped briefly to the trio, but mostly they focused on Chase. "I'd like to ask you a few questions, please."

Sophie glanced at the raging fire and bit her lip.

"Of course," she managed, keeping firm hold of Chase's hand.

They moved a few steps away. More police and firemen arrived, erecting barriers and keeping the growing crowd back. The first officer recorded her name, address, and her account of what had happened. But a few questions turned into a barrage — not just from one officer, but a second and then a third. Sophie had to repeat what had happened over and over, and she found herself tearing up. Coco had jumped into her arms, shaking with fear, and Sophie could relate all too well.

"Did you notice any unusual activity this morning?"

She nearly snorted. Other than the explosion that could have killed her?

"What is your role, sir?" they asked Chase, who growled a curt reply.

"I heard the explosion and came running."

Sophie squeezed his hand. Chase made it sound so simple. But she'd never had anyone come running for her before.

"Did you notice any odor or anything out of place?" the police pressed on.

"Are you sure you didn't see anyone?" another asked.

She did her best to answer, but the questions were relentless, and it felt like all those sirens were wailing at her. Chase stood at her side, looking like he was about to snap, and she was afraid what might happen if he did. Dell had been ordered to one side, and the questions went on and on until one of the officers went a step too far.

"Did you adjust or otherwise tamper with the cylinders this morning or at any other time?"

Sophie's mouth fell open. "Tamper? What are you suggesting?"

The policeman — a big, sunburned *haole* — blinked and took a step back.

Sophie stuck her hands on her hips. *No, I'm not a pushover,* she wanted to bark. *I'm just trying to be nice. But push me too far, and this is what you get.*

Even Chase whipped his head around, and for a moment, Sophie felt on top of the world. But then her gaze caught on the burning wreckage of the smoothie truck, and she wanted to crumple to the ground. The truck was destroyed. It was a miracle no one had been hurt. But, still. That fire was a menacing, evil thing, and it was scarring Lahaina's beautiful landscape. Was it her fault somehow?

Luckily, a female police officer — a beautiful islander Sophie recognized as a friend of Chase's — stepped up with a bolstering smile. "I'm Officer Dawn Meli. Guys, let me handle this."

The other officers backed away, giving Sophie some breathing room. Chase relaxed a tiny bit too.

"Okay, take a deep breath," Officer Meli said. "And start at the top. Just one more time, I promise."

It was easier talking to Officer Meli, who actually seemed to listen when she spoke. When Sophie finished, Officer Meli mulled over various scenarios.

"Could it have been an accident?"

Sophie considered. Theoretically, yes, but the truck and all its systems were inspected regularly.

"Foul play? Are there any competitors in the business?"

Sophie frowned. There were a few. But someone who'd stoop to such violence? "Not that I know of. But I guess you'd better ask the owner, Mr. Lee."

Officer Meli jotted a note then lowered her voice. "What about you? Have you had any trouble? Any threats?"

Chase clenched his fists. "Why would anyone target Sophie?"

Officer Meli put up her hands. "I'm not saying that's the case. But I have to ask. Anyone out for revenge for something?"

Sophie blanched but searched her memory. "No. No way."

"An ex-boyfriend who might feel snubbed?"

In a previous life, Sophie might have thought, *I wish.* But ever since she'd met Chase, her only wish was for more time with him.

She shook her head, and Officer Meli pressed on. "What about money? Any trouble there?"

Sophie's gut twisted. Money? She'd been avoiding that topic for a while, not quite ready to deal with some news she'd recently received.

She answered carefully. "I don't owe anyone, if that's what you mean."

When Officer Meli nodded and went on, Sophie exhaled. After a few more questions, Officer Meli snapped her notebook shut. "All right. That's it for now. Thank you for your cooperation. We'll need you to come to the station for a full report this afternoon."

Sophie's stomach sank. A report even fuller than the one she'd just given?

But Officer Meli smiled, promising it wouldn't be too bad. Then she turned to Chase. "Will you take care of her?"

Was there a hint of a tease in the officer's voice? Sophie couldn't tell.

"You bet I will," Chase grunted, making Sophie go all warm inside.

Dell came over with the dogs then, laughing as Darcy strained at his leash. "You got yourself a real tiger there."

Sophie hugged Darcy, hoping he hadn't bitten anyone.

"I need the car keys." Chase held out his hand.

Dell looked about to question that, but Chase growled, and Dell raised his eyebrows in a question. "You sure you got this, man?"

Chase took the keys and gripped Sophie's hand firmly. "I've got this, all right."

He made a slight gesture, and the dogs fell in step, all following their alpha, as it were. Sophie followed too, still shaky in the knees. Chase whisked her right through the crowd and past several reporters who might have hounded her if it hadn't been for Dell, one step behind.

"I saw the whole thing," he announced loud enough for everyone to hear. "Ask away."

Everyone's attention jumped to Dell, and Sophie exhaled in relief. Chase glanced back with a sigh. "Yeah. Dell is good at that kind of thing."

"Well, thank goodness for him," she said. Then she covered Chase's hand with both of hers. "But most of all, thank goodness for you."

He beamed then tugged her forward against the flow of curious onlookers headed toward the fire. A short time later, they arrived at his pickup.

"Where to?" he asked.

She blinked a few times. First of all, at the truck. Sometimes, Chase drove a fancy red Ferrari. Other times, he drove this battered Toyota pickup. The funny thing was, he didn't seem to notice the difference, and she loved him for that. Well, she loved him for a lot of things.

Slowly, she forced herself to focus. Where did she want to go? Home or to her quiet, thinking place? And, wait — there was Chase to think of.

"What about work?"

He tilted his head. "Work?" He didn't actually say, *I hate to mention it, but your job just blew up,* but his eyes suggested as much.

She laughed. "No, I mean your job."

He shook his head. "Dell will find someone to cover for me."

She studied him for a second. It would be nice to have friends who would jump to your assistance at the worst — or best — of times. But then her eyes drifted to the dog tags hanging around Chase's neck. Dell wore a set too. She had never asked exactly where they'd served and when, but it was clear they'd been through a lot together.

Chase stood silently waiting for her answer, and her heart swelled again. He was so quiet. So steady. So eager to help. What had she done to deserve him?

Then she cleared her throat. "Would you mind driving a little way up the coast?"

His look said he'd drive to the moon and back for her, and she fell in love all over again. Then he leaned down, picked up Boris like a sack of potatoes, and placed him in the bed of the truck. Coco jumped at Sophie's knees, begging to join in. Meanwhile, Chase turned to Darcy, who growled.

"Growl all you like, little guy," Chase murmured. "I'm the boss here."

A second later, a grumbling Darcy submitted to being scooped up by Chase and being placed in the back. The little terrier didn't dare bite Chase, but his dignity was clearly hurt.

"Good dog." Sophie petted him while securing each leash. "You're my good dog."

That seemed to help, and a minute later, she, Chase, and the dogs were cruising up the highway, heading north.

"You live here?" Chase asked after a few miles ticked by.

She waved over her shoulder. "No, back there. But if you don't mind the drive..."

"I don't mind," he said quietly.

With every mile that passed, Sophie relaxed a little more. Chase did too. Were the turquoise water and pure blue sky as soothing to him as to her? Did he enjoy that feeling of open space as much as she did? Hotels and condos choked the first part of the coast, but once they passed the high-end resort at Kapalua Bay, it was all open country again. On Maui's inland, *mauka* side, the slopes climbed higher and higher, reaching into a veil of clouds. Out to the *makai* side was the beautiful scoop of Honolua Bay, and out in the distance, the long, sleek shape of Molokai.

The road dipped and turned, and just when Sophie was thinking of asking Chase to pull over for a moment, he hit the blinker and did exactly that.

"Okay with you?" he asked.

"Perfect," she whispered, looking out over the ocean. A tangle of wild roses stood beside the pickup, and she could smell their heavenly scent. Beyond them, the Pacific stretched to a hazy, faraway point where she couldn't tell water from sky any more.

"This is why I came to Maui," she whispered.

Chase cocked his head and waited exactly the way the dogs did when she had no one else to talk to.

She waved vaguely. "The beauty. The peace. A reminder of everything positive in the world."

To her relief, he didn't ask what that might be in contrast to. He just nodded as if he knew precisely what she meant.

"What brought you here?" she ventured a moment later.

Chase, as always, contemplated his words before committing to exactly two. "A job."

"At the Lucky Devil?"

He laughed, and a little bit more tension slipped away from them both. "No, that's just a side gig. I work security at a private estate."

She'd heard as much, but she wasn't sure it was true. Did that explain the Ferrari?

A dozen questions bounced around her mind, but she didn't utter one. Did it matter where Chase lived or what kind of car he drove? All she really cared about was him. The real him.

"Do you like it here?" she asked.

He pursed his lips and looked off into the distance. "I like it well enough."

For a moment, she thought that was it. But miracle of miracles, Chase expanded on that thought.

"When we first got here, all I wanted was to go home to Montana. But then..."

She waited the way he waited when she spoke. But that seemed to be all, so eventually, she prompted him. "Then what?"

His Adam's apple bobbed, and he looked at her, then at the floor, suddenly shy.

"Then I met you."

A dozen white doves might have fluttered around her heart for all she knew — that's what his words did to her. Her breath caught as she gazed into his eyes. "I'm really glad I met you."

"I'm really glad too," he whispered.

It was one of those perfect, *on the cusp of something amazing* moments they often shared. If only she could figure out what to say from there.

Chase, I really like you. That would be a good start, but her throat closed up, and she couldn't speak. Not even to ask, *Do you like me?*

Well, he must like her. He'd agreed to a date, after all. But part of her mind still refused to consider herself worthy of such a sweet — not to mention sexy — guy, and doubts welled up all over again. Still, the way he looked at her — really *looked*, like she was a flower worthy of painting — said, *Sophie, I really like you too.*

Her spirits soared, and she smiled, feeling more beautiful than she'd ever been. The front seat of the pickup wasn't that wide, and it was all too easy to picture herself sliding over and kissing him.

And, whoa. Nearly getting killed must have freed her inhibitions, because she really was sliding over to kiss him. It was as if she'd hastily penned a bucket list and had to tick off as many items while she could. Number 3, *Stop and smell the roses.* Number 2, *Spend time with the people she loved.* Number 1, *Kiss Chase...*

Chase inched closer as well, and before she knew it, their noses were brushing in a prelude to a kiss. For a moment, they both paused, savoring the sweet innocence of that Eskimo kiss. Then Chase's lips twitched, and Sophie started closing the distance again, when—

Zoom! An eighteen-wheeler rushed by, making the pickup bounce. The dogs exploded into frantic barks. Chase and Sophie broke apart, turning toward the commotion.

"Sorry," Sophie murmured, hiding her crimson cheeks. "They get a little loud at times."

Chase looked at her wordlessly, and all kinds of emotions rushed through his eyes. Yearning, like he had longed for that kiss with all his heart. Regret, for having missed his chance. Resolve, to make it up as soon as he could.

Then he cracked into a tiny smile that said, *Next time.*

Sophie smiled back. *Next time* was right.

Chase chuckled, and just like that, the awkwardness passed.

"Barking is the best part," he said. "That and riding in the back of a pickup."

She grinned. "You sure know dogs."

Chase cleared his throat and started up the vehicle again. "I guess you could say that."

He drove on, following the coast. The road narrowed a short time later, becoming a winding one-laner that kept most traffic at bay. The scenery grew wild and more tangled, and cars were few and far between. When they eventually reached mile marker thirty-eight, Sophie waved for Chase to pull over.

"Nakalele Blowhole," he said, recognizing the spot.

She nodded. "I love it out here."

It was a raw, rocky place — not one most people would put on a list of Maui's best. But there was space and enough solitude to make it a good place to think.

The dogs pranced around the back of the pickup, excited to explore. Sophie let them out, and Chase fell into step behind her as they all followed a winding path to the rocky coast. The wind yanked at Sophie's shirt and hair on that harsher, more exposed side of Maui. But something about the place kept her coming back again and again.

She whistled, making sure the dogs stayed close, and headed to a rock several hundred yards away from the blowhole. Near enough to watch and wait for it to spout, but far enough to have some space to herself, what with the handful of visitors drawn to the sight. She settled down on the rock, listening to the waves crash against the shore. Every few minutes, the blowhole would spout like a whale coming up for a breath, covering the area with a fine mist. Chase sat beside Sophie, and she concentrated on his comforting presence.

"You sure you're okay?" Chase whispered after some time.

She nodded, but a second later, tears stung her eyes as it hit her all over again. The dogs had been trying to warn her, but she hadn't listened. She could have been killed, and the dogs too. Or worse, horribly burned. Then there were Officer Meli's questions, which still swirled around her mind.

Have you had any trouble? Any threats?

Not that she was aware of. But suddenly, she wasn't so sure. She'd left home on bad terms, which wouldn't have been a big deal if she'd come from a normal family in a normal place.

"Hey," Chase murmured, scooting over to hug her as the tears became a flood.

She squeezed her eyes shut, trying to lock out the memories, recent and from further back in time. Instead, she concentrated on Chase. His strong, sure arms. His easy silence, allowing her to cry while assuring her everything was okay.

She cried a little longer, getting it all out of her system. The fear. The shock at being questioned like a suspect. The terrible sight of those flames. Bit by bit, the tears carried all that away, leaving her sniffling and chagrined. Slowly, she pulled out of Chase's embrace and wiped her face.

"I'm so sorry. This was supposed to be a nice day."

Chase tilted his head one way then the other. "Maybe we can still make it one."

She closed her eyes, finding that hard to believe. Today was supposed to be their big day. Their first date. Now, it was ruined. "I was going to kiss you and everything."

The second the words slipped out, she smacked a hand over her mouth. Oops. She hadn't intended to say that aloud.

Chase went a little wide-eyed, and her stomach sank. Oh God. What if she'd read him all wrong? Maybe he was just being nice, bringing her out here. He might not even have wanted to go on a date with her.

Her chin dipped, but Chase reached out and tipped it up, making her look into his eyes. A slow, shy smile spread on his face, and he whispered, "Who says you can't?"

Her breath caught as her hopes soared once more. He wanted to kiss her!

"You mean, I can?"

He nodded earnestly and spoke in a scratchy voice. "I'd really like that."

She took a couple of deep breaths, because holy cow, her emotions were all over the place. Not only that, but Chase's eyes were glowing. Or was that further proof of how flustered she was?

She leaned in to double-check, but then she got distracted by his lips. So close. So full. So kissable.

A wave washed over a rock in the distance, making a swishing sound.

So, kiss him, it seemed to say.

A seagull cawed overhead, telling her the same thing. Even Coco nudged her side as if to cheer her on.

So, kiss him, Sophie admonished herself.

She leaned in, closed her eyes, and reached out until their lips met. And, *whoosh!* The blowhole erupted not too far away, making onlookers cheer. Sophie kept her eyes shut and kept right on kissing, though. She couldn't stop. Chase's lips were like the rest of him — tough on the outside but soft inside, and the more she kissed, the more laps those doves around her heart flew. Around and around they went, making her feel dizzy. The good kind of dizzy where you lost track of space and time. The blowhole erupted again, sounding miles farther away, and if she noticed the soft touch of its mist, it was only in a distant, fairy-tale way. All her senses focused on the kiss and how good it felt.

It felt like home. Like a dream. Like a whole new future revealing itself, one enticing glimpse at a time. Chase cupped her cheek, and she opened her lips. Her heart thumped away. Maybe he was right. It didn't have to be a terrible day. She could make it as good as she wanted it to be.

And damn it, she wanted that so badly. More than she'd ever wanted anything.

So she kissed the man she'd been pining for long and hard, just like the past weeks had been for her. Their bodies inched ever closer, and Sophie found the nerve to run a hand over his ribs. She pressed closer, growing more breathless. Wondering just how far she was ready to go.

Pretty far, as it turned out, and she was shocked to find herself sliding her hands down his rear. Nearly sliding around the front too. Chase's touches grew bolder as well, and—

Cries shot out, and they broke apart.

Sophie gripped Chase's hand. "What's going on?"

There was some commotion over at the blowhole. Sophie looked around in panic, searching for the dogs. They were still nearby, thank goodness, with Coco and Darcy rooting around in the scrub, and Boris chasing a leaf in the wind.

"Whoa," Sophie murmured as she realized what had happened. A young man had ventured too close to the blowhole and been tumbled off his feet by the blast. Two friends rushed over to pull him to safety. The trio retreated a safe distance, where they broke into hoots of laughter.

Sophie shook her head. She'd nearly been killed that morning, and she still felt shaky inside. What did those men find funny about near-death?

"Fools," Chase muttered.

There was a sign there and everything. *Warning. Stay clear of blowhole. You can be sucked in and killed.*

"Lucky fools," she added. But really, she was a lucky fool too, considering what had happened that morning. So what exactly did that mean?

She thought it over for a moment, then scooted closer to Chase. When she'd moved to Maui, she'd promised herself to live life to the fullest. To feel beauty, to hope, and to enjoy. That was the moral of the story, right?

Right, she told herself firmly.

Her eyes locked with Chase's, and a moment later, they were kissing again.

Chapter Five

Chase had endured a lot of highs and lows in his life, but he'd never experienced anything like the previous twenty-four hours. He stretched under the cool, crisp sheets and opened his eyes slowly, wondering if it had all been a dream. But it really was the next morning, and he really was at Sophie's house — and in her bed. She was curled up in his arms and everything.

He moved his hand, smoothing the fabric of her sleeve. Yes, they were dressed, because it hadn't been *that* kind of night. He was only there to keep Sophie safe.

Well, okay, to keep her safe and to calm his inner wolf, who'd gone crazy at the explosion. The acrid scent of the burning truck, the flashing lights, the wailing sirens — wolves weren't good with things like that. A decade in the military had heightened his tolerance for that kind of sensory overload, but that was different. This was a threat to Sophie, and it had nearly made him snap.

For the past months, he'd been teetering along the edge of his man/wolf demarcation line. His brothers had been watching him with concern, worried he might give in to his wolf side and go feral again. When he'd met Sophie, that inner struggle had faded away, and he'd never felt more firmly grounded in the human world. But the events of the previous day had hit him like a sledgehammer, and his inner wolf had started its infernal pacing again.

Sophie is here. She's okay, he told his wolf, calming it before it got too riled up. He didn't want to go back to the wild. He wanted to stay in the human world with Sophie.

Slowly, gradually, his wolf calmed down, but it didn't drop its state of alert. The beast was just as restless as Darcy when it came to that.

Chase glanced around, and sure enough, the Jack Russell was standing in the doorway, ears perked, teeth bared, ready to repel any intruder. And the category of *intruder* included Chase, judging by the resentment in the little dog's eyes.

Hey, buddy, he tried. *We both love the same woman. Give me a break already.*

Darcy huffed, and a flurry of ugly images rushed through his mind, all from a hazy past.

Chase shook his head. *That's another man being bad to a different nice lady. It's not me. Look — look how happy Sophie is.*

Still, Darcy didn't let up on that *I've got my eye on you, buster* look.

Chase sighed, wishing he could convince the dog. At the same time, he had no choice but to let out a little more of his wolf aura to put the dog in his place. He respected Darcy, all right. But there could only be one alpha in Sophie's pack, and that was him.

Slowly, he lay back and let his eyes rove around the room. He'd never been to Sophie's place before, and it was nice. Really nice, in a ramshackle, bohemian way. It was a tiny, three-room bungalow high above Lahaina — a worker's cottage from the island's plantation era.

"Look," Sophie had said, pointing out the back window when she'd first showed him around the house. He'd come up nice and close behind her to see. "If you stand right here, you can see all the way up the ridgeline and to the mountain peaks."

"Nice," he'd murmured.

The lush green foliage and craggy mountains were nice, but really, he meant Sophie's scent. Her proximity. The trust she placed in him.

She'd said something about the bungalow being her aunt's, but it sure suited Sophie. The walls were lined with books, and the porch was packed with flowers. His color vision wasn't great, but he was pretty sure they covered every hue in the rainbow. The scent of them tickled his nose even from a distance. Sophie's clothes filled the closet and dresser too — he could tell from the style and the scent. Where the aunt was, he didn't know. All he thought about was Sophie.

They'd whiled away hours at the blowhole the previous day, grabbed a lunch he couldn't remember tasting on the way back, and spent most of the afternoon at police headquarters, enduring further questioning. By the time Sophie was released in the early evening — thank goodness for Officer Dawn Meli, who'd kept things moving — they'd both been worn out, and when they got to Sophie's house...

Stay. Please stay, she'd begged.

She would have had to chase him away with a double-barrel shotgun. But damn, did her words make him feel great.

So, there he was, living out a scene right from his dreams. Well, a scene from *one* of his dreams. He had to admit to having some pretty X-rated fantasies over the past few weeks, and it was hard not to cross that line. For weeks, he'd been burning to touch her. To kiss her. To claim her as his own. And the reality was much harder to resist than the dream. She was so close, so beautiful...

But the instinct to protect superseded everything else, and he lay very, very still, keeping his senses piqued. There'd be no kissing, no letting his wolf get carried away. Now was not the time.

And anyway, a night spent sleeping beside Sophie was a thousand times more satisfying than some of the misguided flings he'd fallen into in the past, thinking that was what humans did. Like drinking coffee, reading the newspaper, or any of the other habits he'd tried and eventually dismissed. But now that he'd found his mate...

He took a deep breath. If it weren't for the circumstances, he'd be in seventh heaven — apart from the fact that Coco had snuck into the bed and lay snoring by Sophie's feet. That, and the fact that he was still reeling from the events of the previous day.

His heart clenched. What if Sophie had died?

He snuggled her a little closer. His arm was looped around the crook of her waist, and his hand lay in the neutral zone of her belly. Her back was flush against his chest, and he wished he could keep her there all day. But there was trouble afoot, which meant he couldn't laze around. There was too much to do, too many unanswered questions to investigate. He had to check in with Dell about work, for one thing, and he also had to follow up with Officer Meli. So he inched away carefully, doing his best not to disturb Sophie, and swung his feet to the floor.

"Morning, Boris," he whispered.

The greyhound gave a few meek taps of its tail.

Chase rolled his shoulders a few times and made a mental note of the book lying on her bedside table — *One Hundred Years of Solitude*. Then he stood, wishing he could wake up the way Boris did, with a long, deep stretch humans so aptly called *downward dog* — butt high, head low, with his spine stretched in a nice, long line.

Later, he promised his wolf.

As usual, he was trapped between two worlds. Among wolves, he was too human. Among humans, he was too canine. Which made him an involuntary rebel who didn't fit into either world.

Around Sophie, though, none of that seemed to matter. For the first time ever, he knew exactly where he belonged.

With her, his wolf agreed.

He took a long look around the bungalow, picturing himself living there. Or even better — picturing Sophie in his place.

She'd love it, his wolf said.

Yes, she would. Not so much for the house, which needed a lot of work, but the surroundings — Koakea Plantation. Ten secluded Maui acres he shared with a handful of shifters he trusted with his life. Hell, he could even trust them with someone as priceless as Sophie. His older brothers, Connor and Tim, had been there for him from the very start — well, the start of his life in the human world. Both had recently found their mates, and Chase figured Jenna and Hailey would welcome Sophie. Dell and his mate Anjali were already friendly with Sophie, and she seemed comfortable around them. Which left Cynthia, the young widow in charge of the plantation. The she-dragon was less outgoing than the others, but Chase was sure she would be okay with Sophie joining them too.

Chase sighed and padded to the bathroom, pausing to look back at her.

His inner wolf wagged its tail. *Mate.*

Even with all the worry on his shoulders, he felt heady and light. Every wolf shifter lived — dreamed — hoped — to find his mate, the one and only woman he was born to share his life with.

Sophie, his wolf hummed happily.

His lips curled into a smile. He'd thought Maui was just another place he'd pass through, not where he'd meet his mate. Funny, the games destiny played.

At times, he sensed that Sophie knew it too. The way her eyes dwelled on his said as much, as did her soft touch and the way she held his hand. They were meant for each other, and that was that. But as a human, she had no clue about shifters. How on earth was he going to break the truth to her?

She likes dogs, his wolf pointed out. *She'll like me.*

Chase scratched an ear. That logic didn't really hold up when it came to shifting. Sophie would freak out, for sure.

But he had more pressing problems to deal with. So he passed back through the bedroom, resisting the temptation to stop and watch Sophie for a while — say, the rest of his life. The dogs all stirred, asking to be let out, so he continued to the kitchen and opened the door. Boris and Darcy rushed out as quickly as the scent of *kahili* ginger rushed in, and he inhaled deeply. There were so many places in the world where a man might wake up with a feeling of dread. Overcrowded cities. War-torn valleys. Barren deserts. Maui had the opposite problem — it lulled you into a false sense of peace. He'd gone outside several times during the night to make sure there wasn't anyone out there targeting Sophie. Everything had been quiet, but that had perplexed him too. What — or who — had set off the explosion? And if Sophie wasn't the target, who was?

"Good morning," Sophie murmured, making him turn.

He caught his breath, as always, when he looked at her. She'd let her hair down for the night, and it had taken everything he had not to stroke it. Hell, he could barely keep from touching her now.

Sophie. His wolf wagged its tail as she joined him at the door.

The morning light glinted off the heart-shaped locket she always wore, and her eyes sparkled with warmth. Her smile was like sunlight filtering through the trees — soft, bright, natural. A gift from God, if a guy believed in such things.

"Good morning," he murmured.

It *was* a good morning, because he got to spend it with her.

They stood gazing at each other, and that was enough for him. But the explosion must have lit some fire in Sophie, because she straightened her shoulders in a *what the heck* gesture and stepped over to kiss him. Right on the lips, with her eyes open and everything.

His wolf rumbled inside. *Maybe she's not as timid as you think.*

He swayed on his feet, caught between a desperate need for more and a paralyzing fear of going too far. Her lips were soft and careful, but hungry at the same time, and her chest bumped his. He kissed back with a tiny, sawing motion she seemed to like, and damn. It was all too easy to picture lifting Sophie onto the kitchen counter and letting her wrap her legs around him.

The kiss grew hotter and deeper, and for a few heated seconds, erotic images smoldered in his mind, so sharp and lifelike he wondered if they were coming from him or from her. But then Coco slipped between them, dashing outside, and thank goodness for that.

He stepped back and gulped for air. What a kiss.

Sophie looked at him through dazed eyes that agreed. *Wow. What a kiss.* Then a blush swept over her cheeks, and the old Sophie was back — the shier, more inhibited one.

She cleared her throat. "Would you like some coffee? Toast? I made some jam."

She opened one of the cabinets that hung above the counter.

Chase's eyebrows jumped up. "Whoa."

Some was one of those words he'd had trouble with when he'd first joined the human world. It could mean three or four, or it could mean a dozen. In Sophie's case, *some* meant shelf after shelf packed with jars. One hundred? Two hundred, maybe? Each had a red checkered top and a sticker that said *Guava*, *Papaya*, or *Pineapple-Mango* along with a date, all written in her neat script.

The red of her cheeks intensified, and she murmured, "Old habits are hard to break."

He tilted his head. What exactly did that mean?

As Sophie moved around the kitchen preparing a quick breakfast, she elaborated. "My family, well... They liked to be self-sufficient."

Chase could relate to that, but Sophie scowled like it wasn't the best memory.

"The thing was, they took it to extremes. My stepfather was always worried about the next catastrophe. Nuclear war. Natural disasters. Communist takeovers..."

Chase did a double take. Communist takeovers?

Sophie sighed. "We always had to be prepared." She opened another cabinet to show that it, too, was packed with supplies.

He shrugged, trying to put her at ease. "Nothing wrong with being prepared."

She made a face. "By stockpiling five years of supplies?"

He gaped. Okay, that was a little much. "Wow. My family was happy to make it from one winter to the next."

Oops. He probably shouldn't have said that, judging by Sophie's curious expression. His mind spun as he tried to figure out how to put wolf pack life in human terms.

"We lived way out in the mountains. We hunted." His nostrils flared as the memories came back — memories of sprinting through the woods on four feet in hot pursuit of a deer. The thrill, the total concentration. "Went fishing." He could feel the cold splash of river water on his belly and see his canine snout cutting a furrow through the surface. "That kind of thing."

Sophie nodded as if that was completely normal, so, whew. But then she asked about his parents, and he hemmed and hawed. How to explain?

My mother was a wolf — pure wolf — in a pack that lived in the Bitterroot Range. My father was a hybrid shifter who could take any animal form. He ran with our pack for a few months. Just long enough to knock up my mom before he took off again.

Unlike most shifters, he'd been born a wolf in a one-pup litter and only started shifting into human form at a few months old — much to the shock of his wolf pack. Staying in canine form was crucial to his survival, but shifting had advantages like being able to release pack mates from traps with his human hands. That had earned him a high ranking in his wolf pack, but still, he'd never quite fit in. His human life had felt the same — except when he was with Sophie. She grounded him firmly in the human world and made him dream of finally finding a place called home.

"My mom liked the mountains. My dad took off when I was young," he said, leaving it at that.

He refrained from calling his dad a total deadbeat and from discussing the *hybrid shifter* part. That would be especially hard to explain. Hybrids were very rare, and their offspring usually took a single animal form. That was why his brother Connor was a dragon and Tim, a bear.

"You have a brother, right? Tim?" Sophie asked.

Chase nodded. "Half brother, but yeah. Like Connor."

Those two had lived with their bear shifter mother, integrated into human society as well as any shifter could be. Chase had only come in out of the wild in his late teens, when his mother had died. Peacefully, thank goodness. There'd been that — and the fact that his human side had been calling to him for a while. Still, the transition had been hell, and not just because he missed his wolf family or had felt overwhelmed by the noise and bustle of the human world. The inconsistency of humans was just as bad. Humans said one thing but did another. They waged war to achieve peace. They admired

Mother Nature but chopped away at her, one defenseless acre at a time.

Still, he'd persevered because he'd sensed destiny steering him onto a path he simply had to follow. Over the next decade, he'd despaired that destiny had forgotten him. But then he'd met Sophie, and that feeling of a guiding force was back and stronger than ever.

She is our destiny, his wolf assured him.

"What about Dell?" Sophie asked, jolting him back to the present.

Chase frowned. Dell was a lion shifter. But damn it. He couldn't exactly announce that, could he?

"We met in the army. Same unit. So he's like another brother, really." One with a mane and a tail.

Chase ran a hand through his hair. How was he ever going to explain to Sophie that those men could shift into animal form at any time?

"Did you all come out here together?" Sophie asked.

He nodded. "A friend offered us security jobs. The good kind, in a nice, quiet place."

That friend was Silas Llewellyn, dragon shifter and owner of Koa Point estate. The other guys had hopes of making the offer a long-term gig, but Chase had been secretly planning to return to his home pack as soon as he could. Ten years of military service had shown him enough of how cruel humans could be. Of course, he had witnessed humans at their finest as well — principled soldiers. Heroic mothers. Farmers determined to make a new start from the war-ravaged earth. Still, he'd had enough. Living in tune with the seasons as a wolf would be simpler and more satisfying.

But then he'd met Sophie, and everything had changed.

She nodded and looked out the window, lost in thought. "That's why I came to Maui. To concentrate on the good in life instead of worrying about imminent disaster. You know what I mean?"

Oh, he knew, all right. Any place that didn't rain live mortars was good.

Then he frowned, remembering the explosion. Right here in his tropical paradise.

Bad man. Mess. Hurting my nice lady, Darcy had said.

Chase finished his toast and stood. "Look, I'd better go. Are you going to be okay?"

She nodded a little too quickly, and he could see the uncertainty in her eyes. But there was grit and determination too — and that, in spades.

Just you wait. She'll show you how tough she can be, his wolf hummed.

Chase wouldn't mind that, but he hoped to hell it wasn't necessary. She'd already been through enough as far as he was concerned.

"Apart from the call I have to make to my boss, no problem." She tried joking it off, but her nervousness showed.

Chase thought that one over. Mr. Lee. Had his business been the target of the bombing, albeit indirectly?

His wolf growled. *How direct does it have to be? Sophie could have been killed.*

In any case, he'd definitely be investigating Mr. Lee.

"Then, I have to go. But listen. You be careful. Call me the second you notice anything that seems off, okay?"

She nodded, looking spooked, which killed him. But he wouldn't uncover any new information from inside that tiny bungalow, so he had to get moving. He did pin Darcy with a stern look, though.

Did you hear that, little guy? Don't let anyone close to her. You got me?

Darcy showed his teeth in a rare sign of agreement. He might not like Chase, but he'd do anything for Sophie.

Anything, the dog's solemn expression swore.

"Hey," Sophie said, stopping Chase at the door. "Did I say thank you? I mean it. For everything."

"You don't have to."

"Oh yes, I do. So, thank you. For everything. And in spite of everything, I had a good time. With you at least."

She might as well have set off a batch of fireworks in his soul, because rays of light filled all that empty space.

"I even got that kiss," she added. "And it was great."

He grinned. "Which one?"

She leaned closer. "Each of them."

He was at a loss how to respond, at least in words. But his legs steered his body closer to hers, and his gaze dropped to her lips. All that yearning she'd kindled in him had to go someplace, right?

Right, his wolf said.

He leaned a little closer, and fire swirled through his blood. Sophie's face was flushed, and her hands touched his sides. Was she as eager for a kiss as he?

Yes, the shine in her eyes said. *Desperately.*

Slowly, ever so slowly, he leaned in, and just as slowly, Sophie reached up. They puckered up at exactly the same time, and the moment they touched, flames erupted in his mind. Not the angry flames of the inferno at the truck. The good kind that made him forget where he was, who he was, and the danger Sophie could be in.

Her lips moved under his, and her chest rose in a sigh. At first, her touch was hesitant, but within the space of a few heartbeats, that innocent kiss took off like a runaway train.

Chase tried to put the brakes on — he really did — but his wolf did the opposite, and before he knew it, he had Sophie pinned against the wall. His lips tugged at hers, and his hands held her firmly, like he never wanted to let go.

It seemed much too rough. Too raw. Too... sexual. But he couldn't stop, especially with Sophie whimpering for more. Her tongue swept over his teeth, and her right leg snaked along his. His wolf howled, and his breath came in short pants. As if caught in a tornado, he lost all sense of up and down, wrong and right. All he knew was how desperately he wanted — needed — Sophie.

Then Coco yipped at Boris, sending him scuttling away from the food bowl, and Chase and Sophie broke apart.

"Wow," she whispered, eyes still locked on his.

He could barely breathe — think — move — except to agree. "Wow."

Destiny, his wolf whispered.

Of course, it was destiny. Sophie was his, and he was hers.

But then he remembered why he was there and what he was about to set off to do. He couldn't let anything distract him from protecting Sophie — not even his love for her.

"Trust me when I say leaving is the last thing I want to do," he murmured.

The corners of her mouth curled up. "It's the last thing I want, too." Then she took a deep breath, as if summoning all her courage, and looked him straight in the eye. "Yesterday, I nearly died. Today, I feel more alive than ever, and that's because of you."

He melted all over again, and the sections of his soul he'd started to shutter off opened up again.

He kissed her hands. "I only started living — really living — when I met you."

And there he stood for another full minute, soaking in every aspect of his mate. Her soft touch. The depth of her green eyes. Her amazing, flower-laced scent. Then, summoning all the self-discipline he had, he released her hands and eased away.

Leaving Sophie was like pulling off a Band-Aid slowly, but he couldn't bring himself to move any faster. It was only when he'd put a few steps between them that he managed to switch over to soldier mode. The part that knew how to get things done even when he didn't want to.

"See you soon," he whispered.

Sophie's fingers brushed over his hand, and her eyes sparked with hope. "See you soon."

He turned to go, but she called after him one last time. "Chase?"

He fought away the instinct to run back. To hold her close and never let her go.

Her voice dropped, and she gulped. "You be careful too."

Chapter Six

Sophie spent the morning gardening around her aunt's bungalow, trying to mentally prepare herself to see the burned-out wreckage of the smoothie truck. She did the same during the long walk down to Lahaina, where she'd left her car the previous day. But the moment she arrived and caught a glimpse of the scene in the seaside park...

She gasped and covered her mouth then took a step back.

It was a good thing she'd skipped lunch, because her stomach roiled. The shiny silver sides of the smoothie truck had become a mottled, ashy mess, and shards of glass littered the road. The bright, flowery logo of the smoothie truck was blistered and covered with soot, with *Sunshine Smoothies* truncated to *Sunshine Smoo*. Instead of drawing customers with its promise of fruity goodness, the truck had attracted a gaggle of gawkers. Sophie stared, sickened, as a tourist snapped a selfie of herself in front of it. Was the woman planning to put that shot in an album alongside shots of waterfalls and palm trees?

"Oh, for goodness' sake," Sophie muttered, turning away.

But that didn't keep the burned odor from filling her nose, nor the sound of idle chatter from reaching her ears.

"How exciting! It blew up," someone said.

Sophie snorted. Exciting? She could have been killed.

"What caused it?" another onlooker wondered.

Sophie pinched her lips. She'd spent most of the night wondering the same thing.

"Arson? A faulty generator? Who knows," someone said.

Foul play? Revenge? Money? Officer Meli's comments echoed in Sophie's mind.

She tapped her fingers against her sides nervously. It would be awfully nice to find out it was none of those things.

Can't trust anyone, anywhere, anytime. The voice of her stepfather joined Officer Meli's in her mind.

Sophie closed her eyes. She had come to Maui to escape that paranoid mind-set. In fact, she'd taken the smoothie job because it helped her make the world a better place, at least in a small way. Was fate laughing in her face?

The sea breeze toyed with a wisp of hair that had escaped her four-strand braid, and she drew a slow breath. No, that couldn't be. Whatever force governed the universe — God? Mother Nature? Destiny? — she had to believe it was crying too.

She turned as a tow truck beeped and backed up to the charred wreck, ready to take it away.

"No," she whispered to herself. She'd come with the vague hope of looking for evidence of something out of place, but she couldn't do that if the truck were hauled away.

A police officer directed the tow truck from one side, and she stepped forward to stop him. But someone moved in the distance, making her stop in her tracks. That red-faced man was her boss, Mr. Lee, owner of Sunshine Smoothies. A man on the warpath, obviously. He came storming right up to her, shaking an accusing finger. No, wait. He stomped right over and clamped a hand on her shoulder. Hard.

Without thinking, Sophie flicked out her hand, jerked her elbow, and—

"Whoa," Mr. Lee yelped as she thrust his arm away.

She caught herself half a second before following that up with a kick. *Whoa* was right. Apparently, some of the training her stepfather had forced upon her worked. Still, Sophie frowned. Defending herself was all well and good. But smacking her boss's arm away?

Mr. Lee stared in surprise then broke into a litany. "Don't you get fresh with me."

Fresh? Sophie wished she could show him *fresh.* But nice girls didn't go around hitting people, did they?

Mr. Lee glared. "Now, tell me what happened. What the hell did you do?"

She was so taken aback, she couldn't utter a peep. Lucky thing a deep voice boomed a reply for her.

"She didn't do anything."

Sophie whirled and spotted Chase stepping up. Her own Lancelot, coming to save the day. They'd gone their separate ways that morning, and she hadn't anticipated meeting him until later. But it was a damn good thing he had come along. Mr. Lee wasn't the easiest person to deal with at the best of times, and now...

"Look at my truck!" he bellowed.

Chase practically growled. "Yeah, look at it. Sophie could have been killed."

He crossed his arms over his chest, creating a menacing image that made Mr. Lee shrink back. But when Sophie looked closely, she could see Chase was practically trembling with rage. Maybe those crossed arms had more to do with keeping his anger under control than intimidating anyone.

She put her hand on Chase's arm, willing him to calm down. "I'm fine. Everything is fine."

"Well, my truck isn't fine," Mr. Lee snipped.

The police officer kicked aside a piece of burned bumper, and it clattered across the road as if to accentuate Mr. Lee's point. The tow truck began to crank in the wreck, and the racket was enough to silence Sophie's boss for a while. Well, his mouth kept moving, but Sophie couldn't hear a word above the whine of the truck. Instead, she focused on Chase, who winced at the noise but didn't budge. She squeezed his hand, grateful for his support, and he forced a tiny smile for her sake. Then his eyes flicked to a spot over her shoulder, and he nodded to someone. Sophie turned and saw Dell waving them over to where he stood.

"Heya," Dell said with his usual smile. With one hand, he smacked Chase on the shoulder. The other hand he kept cradled around the baby suspended comfortably in a snuggler at his chest. "Come on over here, away from those fumes." He cuddled the baby closer.

Dell's partner, Anjali, was at his side, and she took Sophie by both hands. "You poor thing." She'd become a regular customer at Sunshine Smoothies in the two months since she'd moved to Maui to be with Dell. "Are you okay?"

Sophie nodded quickly. Well, she wasn't *that* okay, but what else could she say?

"How can we help?" Dell asked.

Chase growled. "Help me not tear that jerk apart with my claws—"

Dell cut him off with a stern look and a harsh, guttural sound. "No problem. Leave it to us."

Claws? Sophie blinked.

"No," Anjali said as Mr. Lee came storming over. "Leave this to me."

Sophie wondered what Anjali could possibly do. Mr. Lee was furious, and it was all her fault.

"My truck is a total loss. What the hell did you do?" he barked.

"I didn't do anything," Sophie insisted. "I just went out for a second to check on the dogs. . ."

"You left it unattended?" he screeched.

Three steps hardly counted as *unattended*, but what could she say?

"You'd better hope my insurance pays for this," he went on.

Anjali cleared her throat. "Does your insurance cover personal injury claims?"

Mr. Lee stared at her. "What do you mean?"

"You know, in case one of your employees decided to sue," she said, oh so innocently.

"Sue me? For what?"

Anjali shrugged and looked at Dell. "What was it the police suggested? Faulty safety systems?" She tut-tutted. "When was the last time you had that vehicle inspected?"

Mr. Lee hemmed and hawed, and Anjali shot Sophie a *Now we've got him* look.

"I see," Anjali said. "Well, it would be a pity if Sophie decided to sue."

"But she's perfectly fine," Mr. Lee insisted.

Sophie made a face. Yes, she was. Not that it had concerned her boss before.

"Exactly," Anjali said. "And once you assure her she still has a job, I'm sure she'll be less inclined to sue."

"Yeah." Dell clamped a hand on Mr. Lee's shoulder, making him wince. "Why don't you make sure she understands how sorry you are?"

"Sorry?" Mr. Lee snapped. Then Dell squeezed, and he grimaced. "Right. Sorry."

"The important thing is to get back in business," Anjali went on. "Surely, you have another unit you can move to this location."

"It's not that simple."

Dell snorted. "It is a truck, right? As in, you can move it around?" He mimicked a driving motion.

Anjali nodded. "From what I understand, you have an entire fleet."

Mr. Lee did — almost a dozen spread out all over Maui.

"And since Lahaina is such a lucrative spot..." Anjali continued.

"Very lucrative," Dell murmured without releasing his grip.

"...I'm sure you'll have Sophie back to work soon," Anjali said. "Plus — and I hate to say this, but just think — you'll have all that free publicity. Believe me — even bad news is good publicity."

Mr. Lee's eyes took on an entirely new shine. "Publicity, huh?"

Sophie looked between Dell and Anjali. Their good cop/bad cop thing was working. More importantly, Chase had backed down from a look of imminent murder to *I might let this guy live — for now.* And, wow. Did it feel good to have a whole team on her side.

The tow truck revved its engine and rolled away with the wreck, and for a moment, everyone watched. Before long, the only evidence of the accident — crime? — was a charred patch of earth and slivers of broken glass that shone menacingly in the sun.

Sophie frowned. All she really had to go on was the reaction of the dogs. Maybe the explosion had been an unavoidable accident.

But the back of her neck itched as a little voice murmured, *Maybe not.*

"What you need is to get another truck here, ASAP. Plus a reliable employee to run it. Like Sophie," Anjali said.

Sophie held her breath. What would her boss say?

He wavered, but one glance at Chase, who stood there glowering, and Mr. Lee acquiesced. "I might have a spare truck."

"Perfect." Dell smacked Mr. Lee's back hard enough to propel the man a few steps. "How soon can you get it here?"

Mr. Lee pulled out his phone and turned away, leaving Sophie marveling at the persuasive powers of Chase's friends.

Anjali patted her shoulder. "You do want to keep your job, right? If not, I'm sure we can help you find something else."

Sophie closed her eyes. They were all so nice. She had no idea where to begin.

"I don't know," Chase muttered. "What if it's not safe?"

Sophie gave herself a little shake. In all likelihood, the explosion had been an accident. As for her job, she'd be happy to keep it. The customers were nice, the views were great, and the pay — well, it covered her expenses, at least. Not to mention that the location kept her close to Chase.

"I'm sure it's perfectly safe. So, yes, I'd like to work as soon as possible."

Mr. Lee hung up and turned back to her. "I can shift a truck over from Makena Beach in two hours."

"Two hours?" Sophie looked at Dell, who turned away with an innocent look on his face. Wow. Exactly how hard had he gripped her boss's shoulder?

"Do you want a job or don't you?" Mr. Lee snapped.

"Of course I want it," she said on instinct. Everyone needed a job, right? But then it hit her. Technically, she might not *need* the job. For the first time in her life, she was likely to have enough in the bank to cover her expenses... well, for a long, long time. She'd only recently received that news, though, and that new reality had yet to sink in. She wasn't ready to share it just yet — not even with Chase.

She nodded quickly. "I love working at Sunshine Smoothies," she said, though she refrained from adding, *Even if I'd prefer a different boss.*

"All right, then. Be ready to go the minute the truck gets here. I'm willing to give you one more chance. But if anything happens. . . "

Sophie gulped. What if something did happen?

Chase looked equally unsure, but Anjali gave her an encouraging grin, making her feel foolish to turn the offer down.

"Nothing will happen," Sophie said with more confidence than she felt.

Dozens of people milled around the area, but her eye caught on one, and her blood ran cold. She snapped her head up for a closer look. Wait a second. Could that really be. . . ?

But the man disappeared around a corner, and she couldn't be sure. Of course, she was so shaken up, it was natural to fall into the old habit of suspecting everyone. Which just went to show how unreliable her instincts were at the moment.

"Are you sure, Sophie?" Dell murmured.

She gave herself a little shake. "Um. . . yes. I'm sure. It's fine."

At least, she hoped so.

Anjali tapped Dell's arm in a subtle signal, and he looked at her, confused. Then he cleared his throat and backed away. "Right. How about we give you two a minute to talk?"

Anjali led him aside, leaving Sophie alone with Chase. Well, as alone as a woman could be in a public park crowded with tourists and police. Chase looked edgier than she'd ever seen him, and no wonder. She'd already figured out he hated crowds and noise. A relic of having grown up in the mountains, maybe? Or had the explosion brought back ugly memories from his army days?

She took his hand and turned toward the ocean, tuning in to a more peaceful scene.

"You don't have to prove how tough you are," he whispered.

Sophie pursed her lips. Actually, she did. She'd vowed not to let fear drive her life, right?

"Really, it's fine," she said, trying to convince Chase, too. The longer she looked into his deep hazel eyes, the more sure she felt. Not about work or anything in the big, bad world, but about Chase.

I love you, she wanted to say. *I really do.*

Her cheeks heated. Did he love her too?

His eyes flashed, and before she knew it, they were kissing. Lightly at first, then harder, even desperately. Like love was a weapon that could beat back any evil in the world. A ray of hope that could burn all doubt away. She kissed with all her heart and soul, and Chase did the same, holding her close.

In his arms, she felt safe. Content. Complete. But the outside world, damn it, refused to go away.

"Chase," Dell called. "Sorry, man, but my shift starts soon, and we need to talk."

"Talk?" Chase mumbled, barely looking Dell's way.

"Talk." Dell nodded firmly.

Sophie frowned. Dell and Chase were men of action, not words. Given the context, *talk* could have been Special Forces code for any number of things, like *Plan. Investigate.* Maybe even *Seek revenge.*

She kept hold of Chase's hand, reluctant to let go.

"Don't worry," Anjali told Chase with a reassuring smile. "I'll stay with Sophie, and you two will be back together soon."

Her words were a promise, as if she knew how badly Sophie wanted — no, needed — to be close to Chase. Still, Sophie dragged her feet. What she really wanted to do was grab Chase, take him home, and dive back into that kiss. On the other hand, she had to pull herself together if she was going to work soon. That, and she had to walk the dogs, who were waiting for her at home.

She took a deep breath and nodded. "Thanks for everything." She dragged her gaze away from Chase to Dell and finally Anjali, because she owed them so much. Then she looked back at Chase and faked a brave smile. "I'll see you soon, okay?"

Chase was as tight-lipped as ever, but finally, he whispered, "Okay."

Sophie forced herself to follow Anjali. At the same time, she summoned all the energy she had to send Chase a mental message. It was silly, hoping he'd somehow hear it, but she tried anyway.

See you soon. I love you.

Somehow, just thinking it made her feel better, and she stepped away with Anjali. But a moment later, she whipped around, imagining she'd heard Chase whisper a reply directly into her mind.

I love you too.

Anjali tugged her along just then, and Sophie stumbled away on shaky feet. Was she just wishing hard enough to believe she'd heard those words, or had it been real?

"Have you ever felt so close to someone, you can read his mind?" Sophie asked in a hushed voice.

Anjali patted her arm and flashed a secret smile. "Believe me, I get that feeling all the time."

Chapter Seven

Chase shook his head a little, the way he might if his ears were clogged after a swim. Maybe kissing Sophie had been a mistake, because he could barely think straight. Hell, he could barely *see* straight, and all he could smell was her heavenly rose-and-tulip scent. His lips still tingled, and his blood felt too thick to flow through his veins.

Kissing our mate is not a mistake, his wolf growled.

Well, no, but how could he protect her if he didn't find out what was going on?

"You okay, man?" Dell asked.

Chase kept his eyes firmly ahead. Not really, no. But he wasn't about to admit as much. Every time he had to leave Sophie, his soul ached and his wolf howled. So much so that it scared him, because it was getting worse and worse. His wolf was desperate to claim her, and it was becoming harder than ever to hold back.

"Look, she'll be fine. Anjali will stay with her, and Hailey is coming out to help too," Dell said.

At least there was that. He was only parting from Sophie for a little while, and she would be safe. Anjali was a lion shifter, and Hailey, his brother Tim's mate, was a bear shifter. Which meant those two could not only keep an eye out for trouble — they could protect Sophie against any threat that might arise too.

His nerves settled down a tiny bit. It was good to be part of a strong pack. He hadn't even had to ask anyone for help; Anjali and Hailey had arranged to do so without a word.

So Sophie would be all right — for the time being. But Chase couldn't rest until he was convinced the explosion had been an accident and not the result of foul play.

Dell led him up the stairs to the Lucky Devil, where Tim waved them over to a quiet corner table. They weren't there to work, but to convene on what they'd each managed to discover in their part of the investigation so far.

Tim greeted them with a nod, then leaned closer and got right to the point. "You talked to Dawn, right?"

Chase nodded. Yes, he'd spoken to Officer Meli that morning, but she hadn't had much to report. "She said police experts did a preliminary check and found no evidence of a detonator."

His brother nodded. "I had a look too, late last night."

Chase and Dell both leaned closer. They had faith in the Maui police, but no one on the local squad had as much experience with explosives as Tim did.

"And?" Dell prompted.

"Nothing." Tim shook his head. "I couldn't find a thing, which means it was probably an accident. A fluke."

"Probably?" Chase snorted. *Probably* wasn't good enough when it came to his mate's safety. Couldn't Tim see that?

"It would have taken a real expert to set a detonator we couldn't detect," Tim said. "You can spot amateur work from a mile away, even in a wreck like that. And what are the chances that we're dealing with someone with that level of experience?"

Dell looked doubtful. "Targeting a smoothie truck? I'd say not very high."

Chase frowned. *Not very high* hardly equaled zero.

"There's an outside chance someone wanted to damage the business," Dell said. "And obviously, Mr. Lee isn't the nicest guy to deal with. But I haven't come across anything so far — no employee complaints, no strong competitors. No one with the motive to do something that extreme."

Chase studied his drink. He'd come to the same conclusion that morning, though there were a few more leads he wanted to follow.

"What about Mr. Lee?" Dell asked.

Tim snorted. "Bombing one of his own trucks?"

Dell shrugged. "Maybe he wants to cash in on an insurance policy. Something like that."

Chase tensed at the notion and started to stand, ready to rush back to Sophie. But Tim pulled him back down. "That's a long shot. A very long shot."

"Not long enough," Chase growled.

Dell pushed his glass closer, as if Chase could think of drinking at a time like that. "Sorry. Didn't mean to spook you. I'm just trying to think things through. We'll check out that angle, but I wouldn't worry. Anjali is with Sophie, and she's on high alert."

Tim gazed out over the ocean, deep in thought. "We might be putting the cart before the horse, talking about motive. We don't even know if it was sabotaged."

"The dogs saw someone messing around at that end of the truck," Chase reminded him.

Tim didn't look convinced. "The question is, what did they actually see?"

Chase pinched his lips into a tight line. He had to admit it had all been pretty vague. "It's hard to say, but Darcy was so sure about it. Some guy was messing around near the back of the truck."

Tim and Dell glanced at each other then back at Chase. "I'm sure he means well, but didn't Sophie say she thought the sanitation guys were around? To a dog, it's all the same thing."

Chase balled his fists, ready to shoot back, *But Darcy was sure. Really sure.* The same way he felt sure something was amiss, even if he couldn't put a finger on what that might be.

But he could see it in Tim's eyes. His brother didn't believe Darcy. They didn't believe *him.*

"What about you?" Dell asked. "You've walked the site. Any scent of anyone or anything?"

Chase shook his head. He'd studied every corner of the park, using his keen wolf senses to tease out scents and trails. But the park saw hundreds of visitors a day, and nothing stood out, especially not over the acrid scent of the fire.

"Nothing," he admitted.

"Hailey and I checked the park for scents, too," Tim said. "But we couldn't get anything either."

Chase's mood darkened. Bears had the keenest noses around, and his was strong too. "If only we had something to go on. A suspect, a hint." Then he could search for that particular scent instead of grasping at straws.

"All we really have to go on is the dog's memory," Tim pointed out.

"I hate to say it, but isn't Darcy a little messed up?" Dell asked.

Chase ground his teeth. The same could be said about any one of them. Neither he, his brothers, nor Dell liked to admit it, but ten years of active military service had scarred each and every one of them. Maui had gone a long way toward helping them regain a sense of balance, and the fact that his brothers and Dell had found their mates had helped a lot too. And, hell. If Darcy counted as a little messed up, what about himself? He still felt more wolf than human at times.

"What are you saying?" Chase asked, trying to keep the bitterness out of his voice.

Dell put his hands up. "All Tim is saying is there's no evidence of foul play."

Chase wanted to shoot back something like, *What evidence is there for love?* That would make them stop and think. Love was totally irrational, and yet it was real. Just like fear.

Tim must have read his mind, because he nudged Chase's shoulder in reassurance. "It's not that we don't believe you, man. It's just that there isn't much to go on. That, and..." His eyes strayed to Dell, who took it from there.

"Listen, you like Sophie. A lot. We get that. And it's scary as hell to see the woman you love in danger."

Tim nodded grimly. "Believe me, we know."

Chase fought to keep his canines from extending. Did they? Each of these men had been in life-and-death situations with their mates, but they'd never had to deal with a phantom threat.

"What about Sophie?" Tim asked, cocking his head.

Chase creased his brow. What did his brother mean?

"No one has investigated her yet. You know, to see whether there's anyone out to get her."

Dell laughed at loud. "After Sophie? Man, that's like asking who would want to target Bambi. No way does she have enemies. She said as much, right?"

Chase nodded. But, hell. He was starting to wonder the same thing.

Tim shrugged. "Just saying. That's another angle to look in to."

"No," Chase barked.

He hadn't meant to be that loud or that firm, but the sharpness of his voice made both men lean back.

Tim stuck his hands up. "Sorry, man. But think about it. If we want to be thorough about this, we have to investigate her too."

Chase had thought of that. But it didn't feel right to investigate Sophie — not without her permission, at least. Even a misfit like him knew that part of the human social code. She would never trust him again if he went behind her back.

"I'll ask her," he muttered at last.

Dell and Tim raised their eyebrows at each other but left it at that, and a long, awkward silence set in.

"Listen, we'll keep at the other angles," Tim assured him after a minute of quietly sipping at his drink. "But I have to say, if there's no evidence, it's only a question of time before Silas pulls the plug on us spending time on this."

Silas Llewellyn was the dragon shifter who owned Koa Point estate and Koakea Plantation — the big boss, as it were, who kept an eye on broader developments in the shifter world.

Chase raised his eyes in a question, and Tim murmured in a scarcely audible voice, "There's a dragon slayer on the loose."

Dell groaned. "Not that again."

Chase ignored him. Dell had a way of brushing things off, but Chase couldn't bring himself to be as nonchalant about such matters. "Is that a real threat?"

Tim looked grim. "Sure sounds like it."

Dell snorted. "Dragons. Always vying for world domination."

He was only half kidding, Chase knew. All shifters clashed in one way or another, but dragons had a reputation for epic feuds and conflicts that spanned generations.

Tim shook his head. "This is different. It's not a dragon fighting dragons. It's someone — or something — targeting dragons. Taking them out, one by one."

Chase was aware of Silas's concerns, but frankly, he'd been too preoccupied with Sophie over the past weeks to follow the issue closely. All he knew was that the number of mysterious dragon deaths had increased over the years. Was someone targeting dragons as a species, or was there a method to the slayer's madness? Silas had contacts on two continents investigating the matter, so he was obviously concerned.

Dell looked into his glass. "Dragon slayer. Has an old legend come to life, or is it all just bullshit?"

The way he said it made Chase shiver. He'd never paid too much attention to dragon business, at least no more than it concerned his oldest brother. But Connor had never been involved in the ongoing melodramas of the traditional dragon world, and besides, he could handle himself. But things were different now, with Cynthia and Joey as part of their eclectic little shifter clan. Chase thought back to those first, uncertain days when they'd moved to Maui. Initially, his brothers had clashed with Cynthia, but she'd won everyone's respect over time. Cynthia had become a sister to them all, and Joey, a beloved nephew. Which meant that dragon business was Chase's business as much as any developments in the wolf world. Cynthia had never shared any details, but it was clear she was in hiding from some evil force that had murdered her mate not too long ago. Could that have been the elusive dragon slayer?

Chase gritted his teeth. Sophie had talked about escaping from a world full of fear and suspicion. But, hell. It was damn near unavoidable most of the time.

"No one really knows," Tim said. "My point is, we only have so many resources — especially time. And you, bro, are better off saving yourself the trouble of chasing down a phantom bomber who might not exist at all."

Chase swiped at his ear in frustration — that old wolf habit coming through again. "And do what?"

Dell grinned broadly. "Get yourself that woman, for one thing. I swear, I've never seen a man make his move so slowly."

Chase kept his lips sealed. Waiting had been torture, but it had been good in other ways. He had gotten to know Sophie bit by bit, and every moment he got to spend with her was a treasure.

"That, and that other thing," Tim said in a more serious tone.

Dell's head whipped around. "What other thing?"

Chase did his best not to sink his claws into the table as Tim explained. "Chase's home pack back in Montana."

Dell's voice dropped to a grim whisper. "They got trouble?"

Chase made a face. There was always trouble of some kind. But, yeah. This was a whole new threat.

"Poachers," he said, wishing his voice didn't get so scratchy.

Poachers were a regular threat, and wolf packs mourned every loss of a loved one. But this new threat was on an entirely different scale, with a bigger, more concentrated group of hunters exploring the area. A group that went far beyond angry ranchers or drunks taking potshots in the dark.

Those were still rumors, but Chase was alarmed. Wolves couldn't get to the bottom of such things, but a shifter like him could travel the area and investigate. How real was the threat? Who was involved, and why? Then he could think about what measures could be taken to stop the bastards — or worst case, to move his pack to safer territory.

He closed his eyes. Wasn't it selfish to stay in Maui and pursue his own interests when his home pack needed him more than ever before?

Sophie isn't an interest, his wolf snarled. *She's our mate.*

"Crap," Dell muttered, totally earnest for a change. "When it rains, it pours."

Chase grimaced. That was another of those human expressions he didn't get at first. But now, he understood all too well, given the way he was juggling concerns about Sophie, his fellow wolves, and the dragon shifters he'd grown close to.

He guzzled his drink, more to hide the tic in his cheek than anything else. Who was in more danger — Sophie, his home pack, or Cynthia and her son?

He thumped his glass down and rotated it a few times, drawing circles of condensation on the table.

"Whoa there," Dell said. "You trying to drill through the table or something?"

Chase released the glass with an effort and looked out over the sea. He was trying to figure out what to do, damn it. But honestly, he had no clue.

Tim stood and clapped him on the back. "I need to check in with Hailey. Believe me, we'll keep an eye on Sophie for you."

Chase believed him, but somehow, the blind faith he'd always had in his brothers wasn't kicking in.

Dell leaned in. "Hey, man. It's hard, but you'll figure it out. Trust me, you will." Then he, too, stepped away, leaving Chase alone.

Chase spent the next few minutes staring out at the sea without seeing anything at all. Just thinking of the long, winding road that had brought him to where he was and the foggy landscape ahead — not to mention all those balls he was trying to juggle. They were bound to come crashing down somewhere, sometime.

Then he gave himself a little shake and stood quickly, downing the remainder of his drink. He'd leave dragon troubles to dragons, at least until a more concrete threat arose. And as for his home pack — well, he wouldn't be much use to them if he was preoccupied with Sophie. That meant he had to bring clarity to Sophie's case, and soon.

Soon, a deep, earthy voice whispered in his mind. *Before it is too late.*

Chase shivered as he hurried for the door. Was that the voice of fate? And *too late* — too late for whom? Sophie? His wolf brethren? Joey?

He forced himself to take a deep breath and approach things one step at a time. Which would be a hell of a lot easier if he could ignore the sound of a ticking clock in his mind.

Not a clock, his wolf grumbled. *A time bomb.*

His colleagues from the Lucky Devil waved goodbye, but Chase barely registered the motion. He had to get to Sophie, pronto, even if it was just to keep himself sane. After that...

He struggled to fill in that blank, but his wolf had no such trouble.

Hold her. Claim her. Make her mine.

Chapter Eight

"One tropical swirl and a Molokini Special, please."

Sophie nodded to her customers and started loading up the blenders. It was crazy how quickly everything had moved in the past few hours. The smoothie truck that Mr. Lee had ordered in arrived thirty minutes earlier than expected, and she was already back to work. Mr. Lee had stood glaring from the shade of a nearby palm tree, waiting for her to slip up. She hadn't, and when he stomped in to check the register sometime later, he'd let a begrudging nod slip. Sales had been good — much better than they would ever be on a weekday at Makena Beach. That, and he'd seemed genuinely surprised at the number of regulars who stopped by. Sophie was too. The smoothie business was mostly geared toward tourists, but she'd developed quite a following, it seemed.

"Back in the saddle again, huh, darling?" the captain who ran fishing charters out of the marina drawled.

"Good to see you back, sweetheart," said the kind old gent who worked the bar at the Pioneer Inn.

"I'll have the usual, please," said the kind woman who worked in the nearby library.

"Your pick. I know it will be good," said the woman who put a smile on Sophie's face every time she dropped in. She never drank the smoothies herself. She just carried them over to one of the homeless people resting in the park and stopped to chat for a while.

Mr. Lee frowned. "You know all these people?"

Sophie warmed. Yes, she did. If not by name, then by disposition and habits. The bartender walked with a slight limp. The charter captain was trying to quit smoking. The

63

librarian loved Jane Austen, and the woman who sat with the homeless had the most beautiful sparkling eyes. Every one of them seemed genuinely glad to see Sophie back at work that day.

Sophie bit her lip. Maybe the quiet girl behind the smoothie counter didn't go unnoticed, after all.

Smoothies sold at a brisk pace, and her tip jar filled quickly. That was great, because it meant more money for the animal shelter she donated her tips to. Mr. Lee finally drove off, leaving her in peace. From that point on, the afternoon passed as if it were just another ordinary day. Shadows in the park grew longer, and pedestrians ambled happily on their way.

Every once in a while, though, a chill would run down Sophie's spine. And every time a dog barked, no matter how near or far, she would whip her head around. She even circled the truck a few times, checking that everything was all right.

Which was silly, right? Her regulars had proven that the world was full of kind, caring faces. There was no reason to let herself get shaken up.

Until she did.

During a lull in business, she leaned down to rearrange supplies in the lower cabinets. When she stood again, she yelped in shock at the man standing at the order window of the truck. He seemed to have materialized out of nowhere.

"Surprise," he grinned, pleased to have made a grand entrance.

She covered her chest with one hand and took a few deep breaths. Had he purposely snuck up? She'd looked around just seconds earlier. Where on earth had he come from?

Then she looked closer — past the scruffy beard, the longer-than-usual hair, and the ball cap — and all but shrieked. "David?"

He grinned. "Hiya, Sophie."

Her heart hammered, and her cheeks flushed. "Hi."

"That happy to see me, huh?" His smile didn't fade; it just grew more malicious.

"No. I mean yes. I mean — you surprised me," she stammered. Damn it. Why did she let David Orren fluster her every time?

Probably because he'd hounded her all the way across Maine and over to Vermont after she'd tried cutting her ties to home. First, he'd begged her to come back. Then he'd threatened her if she didn't. And just when she thought he'd given up on her at last, he'd sent her that message.

Heya, Sophie. I'm visiting Maui. We really need to get together. So much to catch up on.

She stood perfectly still, studying every detail for some clue. What was he really in Maui for? And was he the same old David, or had he changed?

He was wearing the same type of checkered flannel she'd always seen him in, the usual cargo pants, and his customary combat boots. The same stars-and-stripes cap pulled low, making his eyes hard to read.

"You surprised me," he insisted. Typical David — turning the tables, keeping the upper hand. "Moving all the way out here and all."

He watched her the way a hawk studied its prey. Circling, planning. Plotting away.

"Yes, well," she stammered. "I needed a change. But what about you? You hate leaving home."

Of all the kids she'd grown up with, David was the one who'd always declared he would rather die than leave Maine. To put it more precisely, he'd always insisted he would die *defending their home turf.*

Sophie shook her head, remembering the conversation they'd had as teens.

We're not exactly being invaded, she'd pointed out.

That's what they want you to believe, he'd replied with a totally straight face.

It always amazed her how two kids who'd grown up in the same small community could see the world so differently. Then again, she was the only one who'd seen things differently. Everyone else bought into the paranoid mind-set her stepfather had spread. David most of all.

She'd left home the day she turned eighteen in search of a new start. David, on the other hand, had stayed, throwing himself into the training exercises and boot camps her stepfather had run, all designed to prepare their community for the worst. Judging by the muscle David had packed on since she'd last seen him, he'd been taking those exercises very seriously, indeed.

He studied her closely. *Really* closely, making her skin crawl and sending crazy, panicked thoughts through her mind. What if he was responsible for the explosion?

She tried dismissing the notion, but somehow, she couldn't. David might mean trouble, but he would never threaten her life. Would he?

"Of course I wasn't kidding about coming. Whatever I say, I mean," he said in a way that might have been a joke or a threat. "What I don't get is why you're still here."

Still? Had he expected her to give up and come running back home? Sophie stiffened.

"Oh, you know," she said. David had a knack for turning every conversation into an interrogation, but this time, she was determined to keep her cool. "My aunt Camille lived here. I came out to visit and ended up staying."

He nodded slowly. "Yeah, I heard about her."

Sophie gripped the counter a little harder. Exactly how much did he know?

"Your mom was real upset when she died," David said without the slightest note of sympathy in his voice.

I was really upset too, Sophie nearly replied.

"Your mom was real upset about the inheritance, as a matter of fact," David went on, studying her reaction closely. "You know, that her sister had gone and left all that money to someone else."

Sophie did her best not to give anything away, but her cheeks heated. "Well, people can do anything they want with what's theirs."

David made a face. "That money would go a long way toward our cause, you know."

Your cause, she wanted to say. *I escaped that nuthouse years ago.*

Then she caught herself. She'd grown up with David. Shouldn't she give him the benefit of the doubt?

No, a little voice warned.

"I was sorry to hear about your father," she said.

He shrugged. "Well, you know. When it's time, it's time."

Her jaw dropped. He was talking about his father, for goodness' sake. Worse still, his father had been one of the more moderate voices in their group.

"Who's leading things now?" she ventured.

His smile stretched. "My uncle Roy."

She blanched. So much for moderate.

"Oh. And how is Barbara?" She'd heard David had started dating, which would mean she was off the hook, right?

But he just shrugged, uninterested. "She's fine, I guess. I don't see her much any more. Not seeing anyone, in fact." He grinned with a glint in his eye.

Sophie held perfectly still. Did David even realize he'd done something wrong when he'd forced a kiss on her, way back when?

Come on, you know you want it. He'd grinned before sweeping his tongue over her lips for a second time. If someone hadn't walked past at that very moment, who knew how far he might have gone?

Her stomach churned as she relived all the occasions she'd avoided him after that, and the time she'd finally worked up the nerve to say she wasn't interested.

Oh, I get it. You want to take it slow, he'd said, nodding along.

No, she didn't want to take it slow. She didn't want him at all.

David was one reason she'd left Maine. But he'd followed at intervals, never quite giving up on her. He'd tracked her to the Vermont farm where she'd found work — and some semblance of peace — and several times since then. The last time she'd seen him was two years previously, and she'd thought she'd finally shaken him.

But now David was back — and creepier than ever.

Her hand strayed to her locket, and as she toyed with it, the feeling of looming danger grew.

"How have you been?" she asked, buying time.

He grimaced. "Oh, you know. Working hard. Fighting hard. Watching the world go to shit all around us."

And off he went on his usual litany of complaints.

"Those fools in the statehouse — not to mention Washington..."

His list started there and went on and on. The government was not to be trusted. Conspiracies were everywhere. Industrial giants were plotting against ordinary guys like him. The tax system was riddled with corruption, and unions were working their usual devilry.

Sophie's pulse rose. So many conspiracies. So many perceived dangers. And David, as usual, was full of overly simple solutions to complex problems he hadn't taken the time to truly understand.

He gestured as he talked, and she caught sight of the necklace that swung briefly into view. Was that a bear claw? Her stomach turned. Wearing animal parts like trophies was bad enough. But that bear claw represented so much more.

"So, as soon as you get home..." he continued.

Sophie had tuned out for a moment, but whoa. What had he just said?

"Home?" She stared at him, confused. Maui was home now.

"Of course, home." He motioned to the singed ground. "I heard what happened. It's not safe for you here."

His words had a cutting edge, and the cloud of fear threatening to sweep over Sophie loomed closer. She hugged herself, determined not to succumb to its gloom. Fear was a powerful emotion and easy to cower from. But there was joy too. Trust. Faith.

She touched the locket at her neck for reassurance.

Trust this. Trust yourself. Trust love, her aunt had once said.

It *was* comforting, somehow. Like a compass, helping her follow the right path.

"Honestly, I'm fine," she insisted. The old Sophie — the one David knew — would have let him steamroll over her and have his way. But the new Sophie — the one she was working so hard to become — could think for herself.

David snorted. "You call this fine? An explosion? You could have been killed."

No kidding, she nearly said. "The police said there's no evidence of foul play."

"Oh, come on." He rolled his eyes. "They only say that to cover something up."

More conspiracies. Sophie didn't know what to say.

Deathly silence stretched between them, and her anxiety grew. Which was weird — around Chase, she didn't mind silence. It just meant he needed time to think or find words, and she loved watching him search for them almost as much as she loved hearing what he had to say. David's silences, on the other hand, came loaded like so many weapons, all armed and ready to blast away. Especially now that she caught him staring at her locket with far too much interest.

"That's new," he murmured.

She covered it with her hand. The locket had no real value, but it had been a gift from her aunt. Just having David look at it made her feel violated.

She looked around and put on her best *I mean business* expression. "Look, my boss could come back any time, and I can't have him see me chatting on the job."

"So get me something," David snapped. His eyes darkened to stormy gray, and he banged the counter with a fist.

Sophie held perfectly still. Maybe she wasn't the only one creating a new identity for herself. David had always been intense, but he'd never lost his cool. Never before, at least.

"Sure." She waved to the menu, glad he couldn't see the tremble in her knees. "What would you like?"

For a split second, he glared as if commanding her to drop to her knees and beg his forgiveness. But Sophie held her ground. This was her turf, damn it. Not his.

David's nostrils went wide, but finally, his eyes flicked over to the menu.

"Fuck, they're expensive. Who the hell buys a drink for seven dollars?"

She shrugged. "Maui is expensive."

"No kidding," he grumbled. Then he paused, clearly waiting for her to offer him a discount, or better yet, a freebie.

Sophie wasn't above handing out the occasional freebie when it was deserved. The little girl who'd fallen and scraped her knee got a freebie, as did the police officer who'd come by one day looking absolutely bushed. She'd also given a free smoothie to the woman whose husband had made an awful scene about something before driving off and leaving the woman alone.

But for David? She kept her lips sealed in a firm line.

"Forget it," he grunted. "Like I said. It's not safe for you here."

She crossed her arms. "Why do you say that?"

"The explosion, for one thing. The people, for another."

Her eyebrows flew up. "The... what?"

David waved around, as annoyed as a man surrounded by a swarm of bees. "The people here. They're a bad influence. The heat makes them lazy. Complacent."

"Lazy? Complacent?"

People in Maui had their priorities straight. Love, happiness, and *ohana* — family — came first.

David frowned. "You need to keep your guard up all the time."

She was about to tell him how much happier she'd become since letting her guard down, when he went on.

"Then there's that guy." David's voice dropped to the bass he reserved for communists, terrorists, and anyone who conspired against the Constitution — whoever that might be.

"What guy?" she asked, stiffening.

"You know, that guy. The one who's hanging around you all the time."

She stared. Did David mean Chase? "Have you been watching me or something?"

David flapped a hand. "Of course I have."

"What?" Her blood pressure skyrocketed.

"Any soldier worth his salt knows to study a situation before putting himself in the line of fire."

Sophie didn't know where to start. Line of fire? And soldier — in what army?

"What situation?" she hissed.

He shook his head like she was the crazy one. "The explosion. That guy. He's former Special Forces. Did you know that?"

"How is any of that your business?" she demanded.

But David went on as if he hadn't heard. "He and his buddies know all about explosives. Detonators. Top secret technology that can't be traced."

She couldn't believe her ears. If it weren't for Chase, she could be dead. And if it weren't for the support of his friends, she would have lost the job she loved.

"He could be using you, you know," David went on in a gritty whisper.

Her jaw dropped. Chase? The most undemanding man she'd ever met? "For what?"

David scoffed. "For your aunt's money. What else?"

She fumed. "How dare you?" She tried to control herself, but she finally snapped, tired of being the one under fire. "Whatever — I don't care. Seriously, David. Have you come all the way to Maui just to deliver unsolicited advice?"

David gave her a confused look that said, *What happened to the Sophie I knew?*

That pushover is gone, she wanted to say. Which wasn't entirely the truth but, heck. She was doing her best.

"I've got business in Maui," David said, without offering any details. "Then I heard about the explosion, so I came to check it out for myself."

Sophie nearly snickered. Good old David, drawn to violence and destruction like a moth to a flame.

"Well, I'm fine." She nearly added *thanks* but caught herself. What did she have David to thank for?

He didn't look convinced. "What are you planning to do with that money anyway?"

Like it was any business of his.

"Honestly? I've spent more time thinking about my aunt and what I miss about her."

"Oh. Right. Sorry," he said, not the least bit convincingly.

"My aunt wanted her money put to a good, peaceful cause," she said, hoping David would get the hint.

He nodded immediately. "Of course. I would do the same."

She rolled her eyes. David's idea of ensuring peace was arming himself to the teeth.

"How much is it, exactly?" he asked.

She frowned. *None of your business* was on the tip of her tongue, but the nice girl in her settled for, "I don't know."

He laughed. "That much, huh?"

She glared. Okay, now she was through being nice. "I really don't know." That was the truth. She'd put off a meeting with her aunt's lawyers because part of her still needed time to mourn. Her aunt — the last member of her family who truly cared about her — was gone. "And to be honest, I don't care."

David looked aghast. "How could you not care?"

"Money corrupts."

David snorted. "Money makes things possible. A means to an end."

She studied him closely. What end? What exactly was David up to these days?

"However much it is, I was thinking of donating it to a good cause," she said.

"Sure." David grinned. "Donate it to me."

I said, to a good cause, she wanted to say.

"For you to do what with?"

He snorted. "Are you kidding? We need to keep up with the times. Do you know what a good AK-47 costs these days?"

No, she didn't. But the sickening thing was, there had been a point in her life when she had known that kind of thing. Growing up among an extremist militia like Maine's Spirit of Seventy-Sixers had taught her many things she didn't want to know.

She looked around, wishing a police officer would come strolling along. Better yet, a small army.

Better yet, Chase, she decided.

Then she drew her shoulders back and tilted her chin up. She'd vowed never to be pushed around again, right?

"Like I said, I have to get back to work. And you must have that business to attend to," she said, looking David in the eye. Nearly cheering at his startled expression, too.

Yes, I do have a backbone. No, I will not cower before you like so many people do.

Never had she come so close to breaking into a sweat while standing perfectly still, but damn it. She held her ground.

Footsteps scuffed to her right, and she glanced up. Within the space of a heartbeat, she was smiling — really smiling, because it was Chase, and the usual burst of joy and light whooshed through her heart. The locket warmed under her hand, and a feeling of peace filled her soul.

Chase smiled back — a big, honest smile that hid nothing. But when his eyes moved to David, his face fell.

Uh-oh, Sophie nearly said. Chase looked exactly like Darcy did before he launched himself at another dog. David was glowering too.

"Chase," she called, using her voice to signal she was okay. Chase had a darker, alpha side. If he thought David was threatening her, who knew what he would do?

"Sophie," Chase murmured in a voice so even, it scared her.

She cleared her throat and decided to try a different tack. "Chase, meet David. He's. . . " She struggled to fill in the blank for a moment. *Crazy? Someone I wish would disappear?*

"An old friend," David supplied.

"David was just leaving," Sophie said, trying to move him along.

David glanced at her sharply. *Since when do you tell me what to do?*

She spread her feet a little wider, happy for the height advantage the truck gave her.

Since I decided to run my own life.

Chase didn't say a word, but he swung his arms away from his sides like a gunslinger getting ready for a fight.

David turned up the intensity of his glare to tell Sophie, *You'll do what I tell you, or else.*

She shook her head slowly and stood as tall as she could. *No, I won't.*

Menacing might not be in her body language, but she sure could do *determined.* To David, everything was about winning or losing. He had to be the winner, which gave him a loser to gloat over. Well, not this time.

Chase, meanwhile, backed her up quietly, giving her time. God, she loved that man.

"I really have to get back to work. You know, the pre-dinner rush." She motioned around as if there really were such a thing.

David scowled and shot a sidelong glance toward Chase in a way that said, *Jesus, Sophie. Are you really choosing that guy over me?*

Yes. In a heartbeat.

Standing still had never been such a battle, but she didn't give in. The locket around her neck felt warmer and heavier than ever, but it added to her confidence, somehow.

Finally, David eased back begrudgingly. "Sure. Right. See you soon?" His clenched teeth and stiff shoulders warned that he was giving her one last chance.

Last chance at what? Sophie wanted to scream. *Just go away.*

Chase cleared his throat, though it came out closer to a low growl aimed David's way.

"I'm pretty busy," Sophie said quickly. "But it was good to see you."

David's eyes darkened, and she wondered what he would do if Chase weren't there.

"Yeah," David grunted at last. "Good to see you too."

Slowly, he turned to go. Then he paused, patted his pockets, and produced a scrap of paper. He scribbled on it and handed it over to her, all folded up.

"Here's my number," he said as if bestowing her with a state secret. "Call me if you need anything."

Sophie stuffed it into the deepest part of her pocket, crushing it along the way.

"Remember what I said," David murmured with a sidelong look at Chase.

Sophie did her best to keep her cool. "Goodbye," she called firmly.

And good riddance, she refrained from tacking on the end.

Chapter Nine

"Old friend, huh?" Chase murmured, doing his best not to snarl at the man's back.

Sophie cleared her throat, but when she spoke, her words came out all warbly. Why was she so nervous around that guy?

"We grew up in the same place back in Maine."

Chase mulled that one over. Old friends didn't have to be good friends, and Sophie sure looked happy the guy was gone.

Well, he was happy too. He'd despised David from the second he'd spotted the asshole crowding Sophie. And then there was that bear claw peeking out from the neckline of David's shirt.

Asshole, his wolf growled.

"Sorry," Sophie sighed once David had moved out of earshot.

Chase cocked his head at her. Why did humans apologize for problems they didn't cause?

Her fingers plucked at her locket or touched the single braid she'd put her hair in that morning. That evidence of distress was the only reason Chase stayed at her side instead of escorting David onto the next flight off Maui. He watched the man amble across the park, and it was weird as hell. David swaggered with confidence, but at the same time, he had a twitchy, vigilant aura to him. Like a goddamn spy or something.

Chase sniffed deeply, trying to capture the man's scent and comparing it to what Darcy had described. But comparing smells was tricky, and he couldn't tell.

The man turned a corner, and Chase looked back at Sophie. "You okay?"

She nodded quickly — too quickly — and wiped the counter at a hundred miles an hour. "Fine, thanks. How are you?"

Humans usually answered that with *Fine* whether they meant it or not, but he couldn't lie to Sophie. So he answered truthfully.

"Better."

Sophie's head popped up. "Better?"

"Sure. Now that I get to be with you."

She laughed, and the motion made sunlight glint in her hair.

Like an angel, his wolf hummed.

"It's always nice to see you," he added. Then he peered in the direction David had gone. "Not good to see him, though?"

Sophie shook her head, and he decided not to push it — for the moment, at least. David set off every alarm in his mind, though he couldn't understand why. He wasn't a shifter, and Sophie knew the guy. Obviously, she wasn't thrilled to see him, but that didn't mean the man was a criminal.

Chase scratched his brow. Now he understood why his brother Connor had been so distracted when courting his mate. Everyone looked like an enemy, making it hard to think straight.

"Mr. Lee got you back in business fast," he said, not comfortable with that idea either.

"Like someone said, you have to get back in the saddle after getting bucked off, right?"

Chase pondered that one. Getting back in the saddle made sense if you were sure the horse wasn't out to kill you. And that still hadn't been determined.

"Listen, Sophie." He shifted from foot to foot. Investigating strangers was easy. But investigating the woman he loved felt like too much like betrayal. "I hate to ask, but about what Officer Meli said... Is there any reason anyone might be out to hurt you?"

Her gaze slid in the direction David had gone, which nearly made Chase sprint after the man with his teeth bared. But she shook her head a moment later.

"I can't think of anyone."

He wanted to ask about Mr. Lee, but he didn't want to unsettle her any more. Dell was off investigating that angle, and Chase couldn't believe Mr. Lee would rig a second explosion so close to the first if, indeed, he was guilty of sabotaging his own truck. A long shot, as Tim had said.

"But..." Sophie murmured, making Chase's head snap up. "But?"

"I suppose someone could be after my aunt's money."

He frowned. "The aunt who's place you're house-sitting?"

Sophie bit her lip. "She died recently."

The way her voice cracked made his heart clench. He knew all about losing family members. Like his mother, who had curled up to sleep one cold winter's night and never woken up. At least she'd died peacefully at a ripe old age, and among family. But she was the exception. Deaths were all too frequent in his pack, and the wave of poaching had only made things worse. Another reason for him to go home, and another reason he felt more torn than ever.

He reached out for Sophie's hand. "Sorry to hear that."

For a moment, he didn't say anything, and neither did Sophie. The world shrank down to just him, her, and the gradually setting sun. Grief welled up out of nowhere, and for a brief time, he wallowed in it. All those pack mates, lost in an ongoing battle for survival. All the men he'd served with who didn't make it home. But when Sophie squeezed his hand, the grief faded, and light poured back into his soul, balancing things out. Life had some pretty shitty moments, but there was a lot of good too. Especially when he had someone to share it all with.

Would be even better to have her as our mate, his wolf pointed out.

As if he hadn't thought of that.

"Thanks," Sophie whispered. Then she took a deep breath and went on. "My aunt Camille was always there for me, no matter how crazy things got at home. In fact, she was the one who encouraged me to come out here and live my life the way it should be."

A mynah fluttered overhead, and they watched it dart across the ever-deepening blue of the sky.

"She left me. . . well, some great memories." Sophie smiled then frowned. "And some money to take care of. So I guess greed would be a possible motive. But I can't imagine that anyone I know would be willing to kill for money."

Chase shrugged. "Depends how much."

Sophie looked as if she'd pondered that question for a while. "That's the thing. I don't know."

He squinted at her. Humans had wills and lawyers and stuff, right? "You don't know?"

She sighed. "I'm supposed to see a lawyer about it, but I keep putting it off. Kind of stupid, huh? It's just that money isn't what I think of when I think of my aunt."

Chase shook his head. Stupid? It just made him love Sophie even more.

"I think about love," Sophie went on. "Joy. The way she celebrated the beauty in the world. She never really cared about money — not for more than the basics, I mean."

Chase nodded slowly. He got that. But a lot of people didn't. Money didn't make you happy, and it didn't solve problems. "Do you think it's enough for someone to kill for?"

Sophie drew her lips in a tight line. "She was a pretty successful artist. Maybe I should find out, huh? Sooner or later, I have to anyway."

She didn't look too happy about it, but yeah. Chase nodded. "At best, that might help us eliminate the possibility."

Sophie grimaced. "And at worst?"

He shrugged. "You'd find out who was cut out of her will, maybe?"

Her face scrunched up in thought, and again, her gaze drifted in David's direction. "She didn't have children, so there's no obvious heir. She said she trusted me to decide what to do with it." She twirled her hair in that habit he loved, mainly because it made him imagine being able to do it for her. "I guess I need to get my head out of the sand and see the lawyer, though."

Chase chuckled, and she glanced at him.

"What?"

He waved a hand. "It took me forever to get that expression."

She laughed, and it felt good to break the tension.

A young couple walked up, and Chase stepped aside, giving them space. Sophie had to finish up her shift, after all. He walked a lap around the new truck, checking it closely, finding nothing out of the ordinary. Hating the mystery of it all over again.

Sophie tended to several sets of customers — enough to keep her busy for the next half hour. Chase used that time to go over every inch of the park and study the smoothie truck from all angles before the sun set, hoping for some clue that would either put him at ease or help him understand where to turn next. Should he investigate David? Or maybe Sophie's aunt?

While the gears of his mind spun, he observed the comings and goings around the truck. One corner of his mouth curled up. That smoothie truck was a microcosm of all he loved and hated about humans. He loved the way customers smiled at the simple pleasure of a fresh, fruity flavor, and the way they sang out their thanks. He hated impatient visitors who barely thanked Sophie for her trouble, but he loved the customers who took the time for a kind word. One woman bought a smoothie and carried it over to an older man she didn't appear to be with, just because.

Humans, his wolf huffed.

Chase nodded. Humans were so hard to figure out. They were capable of incredibly selfless acts, but they could be cruel at the same time. He'd seen plenty of both — even in war-torn regions where tiny gestures of goodwill had rekindled his faith in the world when he'd needed it most. But the bad often outweighed the good, and it was hard to keep the faith.

"The world needs more Sophies," he whispered to himself.

His inner wolf growled. *We need our Sophie.*

He clenched his jaw, determined not to give in to the beast's greed. Protecting Sophie was his priority, not wooing her. So he went back to surveillance mode. When business hit a lull, he stepped to the side door of the truck, and Sophie came over with a look of surprise.

"Uh. . . knock, knock," he tried.

She smiled. "Who's there?"

Chase's stomach knotted as he was hit with the desperate wish to tell her the truth. *Wolf.*

Then she'd ask, *Wolf, who?*

And he'd reply, *The wolf who loves you.*

He cleared his throat. Man, oh man. Connor was right. Love made a man think the craziest things.

"Um, just me. Mind if I check the inside?"

Sophie's grin faded as she realized what he was after — namely, checking the truck over for safety hazards.

"Sure," she murmured, giving him space.

He followed the propane line through all its connections and switches as Sophie looked on.

"Mr. Lee was a little late in getting the last truck recertified, but I can't think of anything that looked worn or out of place."

Chase stood and scratched his brow. "Sorry. I didn't mean to make you think about it again."

"It's fine," she said, though her twisting hands said she was anything but.

There wasn't a lot of space in the truck, what with cabinets and counters crowding every inch of the place, which meant he and Sophie had to stand close. Nice and close, if he had to admit it.

"Really fine?" he asked.

Her eyes brightened, and a second later, they were both grinning at each other like a couple of kids.

Why, Mr. Hoving, her raised eyebrows said. *Are you flirting with me?*

Wolves didn't know much about flirting but, heck. Maybe he'd been in the human world long enough to pick up on a few things. Not that he'd ever been inspired to flirt with anyone before.

"Well, I could be finer," she murmured in a singsong kind of way.

Now, she was the one who was flirting. Chase grinned and inched a little closer. With Sophie, it was impossible to stay away.

"How?" he whispered.

She blushed furiously before working up her nerve to answer. "Maybe a kiss would help." She hunched a shoulder as if to hint it was all the same to her, but he could see her eyes brighten with hope.

A kiss would definitely help, his wolf murmured.

He took a deep breath. Every time he got close to Sophie, desire got the better of him, and it was getting harder and harder to keep his inner beast under control.

Just one little kiss, his wolf urged, all too innocently.

One little kiss couldn't harm anyone, he decided, leaning a little closer. Closer. Closer. . .

He kept his eyes open, but Sophie had hers shut, and he marveled at her trust. Then their lips pressed together, soft as silk, and his eyes shut too. He surrendered to the sensation, while his wolf made all kinds of happy, purring sounds.

Technically, wolves didn't purr but, hell. What else could that tickle in his abdomen be?

He moved his lips over hers, trying to keep it slow. But Sophie was as hungry as he was, and when her mouth opened under his, he couldn't help but sweep his tongue over hers. His hands strayed up her sides, and he savored the way she inhaled, making her chest expand. A bird sang somewhere, and the surf crashed on the beach, but he gradually lost touch with the world around him and concentrated on Sophie. Her skin was so soft. Her curves were so perfect, and her scent and flavor were the most delicious things.

Sophie's hands played over his ears and neck, making his wolf hum with pleasure.

Heaven, the beast murmured. *Heaven is my mate.*

It was heaven, and he never wanted to let her go. But a sharp whistle burst into their world, and a man chuckled not too far away. They broke apart, blinking.

"Don't mind me. Love comes before smoothies every time." The man at the counter smiled.

Sophie blushed furiously. "Oops. Sorry, Hal."

The man beamed, and it hit Chase all over again — the joy that came of tiny gestures, like the pretty girl at the smoothie truck remembering your name.

"No worries, sweetheart," the man said. "I'll come by tomorrow."

But Sophie had burst into action by then, tossing sliced fruit into a blender and making it whirl. Her cheeks still burned with a blush, and Chase couldn't help but feeling a stab of pride, knowing he'd been the one to make her blood race.

Before long, the man had his smoothie, and Sophie had yet another greenback in her tip jar.

"You make sure you treat her right, you hear me?" Hal pointed sternly at Chase.

He stuck up his hands. "Yes, sir."

His wolf growled inside. *Of course I will.*

The man left with a wink, and Sophie held up her blender, giving it a shake. "Look — there's some left over. You want a sip?"

It was crazy, the way her words made his wolf wag its tail.

"You can have it," he said.

She pulled out a tumbler to pour the smoothie into. "We'll share."

She held the blender jar a little higher to pour, but the second she did, a whistling sound zipped by Chase's ear.

Incoming, his wolf screamed.

The glass shattered. Juice splashed. Sophie yelped.

"Get down," Chase yelled as survival instincts kicked in. He hit the deck, taking Sophie with him.

"What the—" she started, then grunted as they fell. Then she stared at her hand. The handle of the blender jar was intact, but the rest was a jagged wreck.

Chase crouched over her, straining to hear.

"Bullet," he hissed, pointing at the casing lodged a millimeter away from where she'd been standing. A .308 if he wasn't mistaken.

Sophie's mouth opened and closed like that of a fish gulping for air. "But... but... "

"Silenced sniper rifle," he whispered, kicking the door shut as his mind spun.

Kill him. Get him, his wolf howled.

Chase stayed low. *Him* meant the shooter, but who exactly had that been? The sun was just starting to set, but there was enough light for a sniper to aim a second shot. He listened intently, considering his options. His wolf wanted to tear outside and hunt down the gunman, but that would leave Sophie vulnerable. The truck provided a degree of cover as long as they stayed low, as did the public space of the park. No gunman would march across a public lawn to finish what he'd started. Still, that didn't mean Chase was ready to peek out the service window of the truck anytime soon.

"Oh God," Sophie mumbled, staring at the casing lodged in the wall. "Someone really does want to kill me."

Chase followed her eyes to the shell. That, or someone was warning her.

Warn her about what? his wolf demanded.

His gut twisted. *Warn her away from me, maybe?*

The first suspect to spring to his mind was David, but what was the likelihood of a guy visiting an old friend and then shooting at her, all within an hour? Then there was Mr. Lee, but he didn't match the profile of a sniper in the least. Still, it was impossible to tell. Humans were tricky like that.

With his left hand, he took hold of Sophie's trembling hands. With his right, he fished his phone out of his pocket.

Sophie's wide eyes darted all over the place. "Are you calling the police?"

He shook his head. "I'm calling my brothers." No one in the park had reacted to the shot — it had been silenced, after all — and somehow, he wasn't ready to trust anyone but family right now. "The only safe place is home."

"My place?"

"No," he said grimly. "Mine."

Chapter Ten

Taking Sophie to his place was a dangerous move, and Chase knew it. It was hard enough keeping his wolf under control as things were. But what choice did he have with a mystery sniper taking aim at Sophie?

"You sure you got this?" Dell had growled, peering into the driver's side of the pickup. He'd come running the second Chase called him in to secure the area. Then Dell had raced the pickup over and kept Sophie covered while she got in.

Chase had nodded once and driven off in a cloud of dust with Sophie clutching his hand. She'd insisted he stop by her house to pick up the dogs, but minutes later, they were racing down the road toward Koakea Plantation.

Sophie rocked back and forth, cuddling Coco. "It was me. It really was me."

He looked at her sharply.

"The explosion. The gunshot. Someone wants to kill me. Why?" she whispered, staring at her feet. "What did I do?"

Chase gritted his teeth. He wanted to know the same thing. He reached for her hand. "You didn't do anything. I mean, nothing bad. You're kind. Friendly. You care in a way so few people do." He squeezed her hand. "Anyway, the question isn't what you did. It's what someone is after, and why."

She shook her head. "I hate this. I hate being afraid. I hate suspecting everyone."

He stroked the back of her hand with his thumb and whispered, "The world is a fucked-up place."

Sophie shook her head firmly, though her hands still trembled. "The world is beautiful. It's just some people who give it a bad taste."

The people part, he agreed with. The part about the world — well, he still hadn't made up his mind.

Coco licked Chase's fingers as if a doggie kiss could make the problems of the world go away.

Chase sighed and pulled his hands away. If only it were as easy at that.

"You mentioned inheriting some money. I know that's none of my business, but that might be the motivator here."

"I've thought that through again and again. If I were to die, the only benefactor is my mother. My own mother, Chase." Her voice rose to a near-screech before breaking off into something closer to a sob, and she shook her head fiercely. "There's no way my mother would hurt me. She loves me, and I love her. She can't understand why I left Maine, but she would never do anything to hurt me."

Chase clenched the wheel tighter than ever, considering who else might be in the picture. But Sophie shook her head so vehemently, he didn't dare ask.

"I'm sorry." She buried her face in her hands. "I can't think straight. I can barely even see straight. I know this is important, but it hasn't really sunk in yet. Do you mind if we shelve this for a while?"

Chase nodded immediately. His brothers wouldn't understand, but there was no way he'd push Sophie closer to her limits. Not tonight, when his primary objective was protecting her.

"You're right," he said, touching her shoulder. "We can talk later."

She shot him a grateful look and rubbed her eyes, almost as if she could rub everything that had happened out of them.

"There's my brother," Chase said, nodding as Connor came out to meet them on his Harley, providing additional support.

Sophie nodded dumbly, but Coco wagged her tail. Did the little dog know a dragon shifter when she saw one?

They drove the next two miles in silence, and Chase had never been so glad to see the turnoff for home. Tim and Hailey were waiting at the gate they'd recently installed at the end of the private drive. Usually, driving past that barrier helped

Chase shut off the outside world, but today... He grimaced. It didn't matter how high their walls stood or how sturdy that gate was. There was always evil lurking not too far away.

"Nice place," Sophie murmured, stroking his hand.

He clenched his jaw. She was the one who'd been shot at, and yet it was her comforting him.

"Yeah," he whispered, glancing over the view. "It is."

In truth, Koakea Plantation was great, especially with all of it bathed in the orange-pink light of sunset. Over the months he'd been there, he, his family, and friends had toiled to whip the neglected property into shape. The plantation house, once a crooked wreck, had become a stunning focal point for the grounds, with space for everyone to meet downstairs. The upstairs had been made into a cozy apartment for Cynthia, the young widow who co-alphaed their little pack, and her son, Joey. Neat rows of coffee bushes had been combed out of the weed-choked slopes, and most of the outlying houses sported fresh coats of paint — not to mention all the improvements inside. There was still a hell of a lot to do, but it was easy to see the place's potential now. All in all, Koakea Plantation was an oasis from the pressures of the human world.

Chase cast a wary glance over his shoulder. If only trouble weren't always half a step away.

"Here. Check this, will you?" he muttered, handing Tim the bullet casing as he eased past. If anyone could glean some information on the shooter from so minor a clue, his brothers could.

"Roger," Tim grunted, looking grim.

"We've got everything set up for you," Hailey called as he rolled the pickup past. "Let us know if you need anything else."

He waved in appreciation, wishing he could find a way to put his gratitude into words. As usual, his entire pack had jumped into action when he needed their support.

"Wow. You guys are really close, aren't you?" Sophie murmured, noticing it too.

He nodded. *All for one, and one for all.* That pretty much summed up a shifter pack.

89

The thing was, wolf packs operated in that principle too, and it gutted him to know he wasn't supporting his kin back at home. He tightened his grip around the steering wheel. The moment he was able to assure Sophie's safety, he would deal with the poachers.

His wolf growled. *And damn, they'd better watch out.*

Images of death and destruction zipped through his mind, and he fought to keep them in check. Anger wasn't a good thing, not for a shifter capable of acting on dark impulses. He had to keep his head screwed on if he was going to help Sophie — and help his wolf pack at home too.

So he took a deep breath, parked the pickup in its usual spot, and led Sophie down the winding path to his home. The dogs followed, huddled closely around their feet.

"Good boy," Sophie murmured, petting one after another. "Good, Coco."

Coco stood a little taller. Darcy still resented him, but Chase could live with that, especially given how vigilant the Jack Russell was. As far as guard dogs went, air-headed Boris left a lot to be desired, but even he was alert.

"Everything will be fine," Sophie murmured, reassuring the dogs. "Everything will be okay."

Chase set his shoulders straighter. God, he sure hoped so.

If he hadn't been carrying a fifty-pound bag of dog food, he would have looped an arm around Sophie just to keep her close. Luckily, his place wasn't too far. Sophie's braid swayed as she walked, and he could barely tear his gaze away.

"It's not locked," he said, motioning for Sophie to let herself in.

She pushed the door open, stepped through, and looked around. "Wow."

The dogs piled in after her, and Chase followed, wincing a little. His place wasn't exactly the showcase some of his brothers and their mates had turned their homes into. It was just a converted barn, and he'd only made a few bare-bones improvements since he'd moved in.

"This is great." Sophie turned in a slow circle.

Chase exhaled a little. He hadn't done much with the ground floor of the barn, but he had covered the ocean-facing wall with windows — mainly at Dell's insistence that wolves needed daylight to keep them from running too wild. That west side of the structure had what Hailey called a cathedral ceiling, which had confused him, because it was a barn, not a church. The east half of the building was split into two levels, with stairs leading up to a loft that overlooked the whole place.

"What a view," Sophie breathed, looking out.

Whew. Chase was glad she was concentrating on that — the burst of sunset colors over the slice of ocean visible from his spot halfway up the hill — and not on how poorly furnished the place was. But, wow. He'd called ahead to warn his friends he was bringing Sophie over, and apparently, someone had dashed in to spruce his place up. The ceiling fan was already turning, keeping the space cool. A vase of fiery Tiger Lilies stood on the crate he used as a coffee table, and an Indian-print sarong covered the worn couch. Someone had tossed a couple of decorative pillows around too. When he threw pillows around, it looked like a mess. When someone like Anjali did it, everything looked nice. Stylish, in fact.

He sniffed the air and caught a hint of Anjali's scent, along with Jenna's beachy fragrance. And — wait. Had Cynthia been there, as well? He followed her scent over to the makeshift kitchen — if you could call the space with a tiny fridge, microwave, and battered steel sink that — and checked the note stuck into a basket overflowing with fancy breads, cheese, and even a bottle of wine.

Just a few goodies to help end the day on a positive note. Kind regards, Cynthia.

Chase read the note three times. Wow. He was going to have to do a lot of thanking when he had the chance.

PS — The cookies are from Joey.

Chase grinned, wishing the boy were there so he could tousle his hair.

"Do you have a dog?" Sophie called, looking perplexed.

He followed her gaze to the pile of old blankets he used as a wolf bed when the urge to sleep in animal form kicked in.

91

"Um, no," he murmured, searching for some way to explain that.

Luckily, the shiny foil of the food basket caught Sophie's eye, and she came over for a look. When she reached for the note, her fingers brushed his, sending warm tingles up and down his spine.

"Gosh. You have a whole tribe looking out for you, don't you?"

Tribe wasn't far off the truth. Too bad he couldn't explain about the shifter part.

"Looking after you, too," he whispered back. That realization touched him just as deeply as the decor and food basket had. His pack wasn't just taking care of him; they were taking care of Sophie as well.

They accept her. They like her, his wolf said.

Sophie looked up at him with those big, soulful eyes, and he ached to tell the truth. The longer he went without telling her, the more he felt like a liar.

He looked down at his feet, cursing himself. He had courage in spades, but that didn't help. He could rush into battle, no matter the odds. Challenge impossible foes. Risk his neck for the sake of his pack. But uttering a couple of words?

"Sophie," he whispered, but even that came out all rough and clunky.

Her hands slid into his field of vision, covering his, and she inched closer. Close enough for her body heat to warm him.

"I need to talk to you," he forced himself to say, even though it made his stomach roil.

"I need to talk to you too."

His ears twitched as he wondered what it might be. Surely, Sophie didn't harbor the kind of secrets he did. The big question was, how well would she take the truth?

He played out different ways of saying it.

I'm a shifter, Sophie. A wolf. And I love you.

Or, wait. Should he start with *I love you* and then get to the shifter part?

"But right now, I don't want to talk. I don't want to think," she whispered.

And coward that he was, he let out a breath of relief.

"What do you want?" he whispered. And, damn. Those words had come out much too suggestively.

Sophie nestled a little closer. Her breath tickled his cheek, and her hands traveled from his hands to his sides.

"Just. . . this," she whispered, sliding her arms around him for a hug.

His arms wrapped around her instinctively, and he inhaled her scent. She smelled so good — all honey-like and homey and. . . and. . .

Mine, his wolf hummed. *Like mine.*

Which felt great, but the bitter scent of fear was in there too, and he hated that. So he held her good and tight, making his chest a shield. He tipped his head down to rest on hers, covering as much of her as he could.

Just let anyone try to harm her, his wolf declared.

The problem was, whoever had targeted Sophie was a coward who attacked from a distance. The hardest kind of enemy to ferret out.

"This is so good," Sophie murmured.

Chase nodded softly. Hell yeah. It was. Especially as the scent of arousal slowly overcame that of fear.

She wants us. We want her, his wolf growled, giving him all kinds of bad ideas.

But Coco kept jumping against his legs, and Boris's thin tail whipped at his shins. Sophie sighed and pulled away with an apologetic look.

"Settle down, guys. Everything is all right." She petted each of the dogs in turn.

Chase studied each, reading their doggie minds. Coco was panting happily, thinking, *Yes, everything is all right because the nice lady says so.* Boris didn't seem so sure, but he wagged his tail shyly at her words. Darcy wore the look of a British Sergeant Major: *So not amused.*

"Maybe we should feed them," Chase suggested.

He grabbed three bowls, and pretty soon, two of the three dogs were munching happily, while Darcy stood between his kibble and Sophie, looking torn.

93

Go for the food, buddy. Chase pushed the thought into the dog's mind. *I swear Sophie is in good hands.*

Darcy's expression said, *That's exactly what worries me,* but Chase ignored him. Sophie was finger-combing her hair out of her braid, and the sight of those long, chestnut locks made his wolf go wild. The ceiling fan whirled, bringing him a whiff of his own arousal.

It's just hair, he tried telling himself. But there was no *just* with Sophie. Everything she did made his pulse race.

"So, you have another room up there?" Sophie asked, looking up to the loft.

Chase held his breath. Yes, there was. His bedroom, in fact. But that only fueled the dirty part of his mind.

"Uh, yeah," he murmured.

"Mind if I have a look?"

His eyes went wide, and Sophie blushed wildly, like she knew exactly what was up there. Another little zing of arousal wafted through the room — Hers? His? — and Chase's wolf wagged its tail.

Of course, you can have a look. As closely and as long as you like.

"Sure," he said as evenly as he could.

The dogs whimpered when they saw Sophie head up, but they didn't attempt the steep, narrow stairs. Chase followed Sophie, preparing to grab his messy sheets and cover the bed. But Anjali, Hailey, and the others had worked their magic up there too. His bed — a queen mattress thrown on the floor — was made up with nice, crisp sheets and covered with a fancy Indian-print sarong. A couple of candles stood on the boxes that served as bedside tables, and the shade of the reading lamp wasn't crooked any more.

"Cute." Sophie smiled.

Chase stared. Cute? Well, yes. For a change.

"The view is even better from here. And, wow. You have a lot of books," Sophie breathed.

One side of the loft faced the west windows, overlooking the swath of lush greens and turquoise blues outside. The other wall was full of books. Crammed with them, actually, all stuffed into makeshift shelves along the unfinished beams. Another couple of piles stood in crooked columns on the floor — books he hadn't gotten around to reading yet. Sophie ran her finger along one row, and he watched her, feeling painfully self-conscious.

"You like reading, huh?" she murmured.

He nodded. Ever since he'd come in out of the wild and learned to read, he'd spent hours flipping the pages of musty books.

"They help me understand," he said truthfully.

When Sophie turned to look at him, her hair cascaded to one side, and sunlight bounced off it.

"Understand what?"

Humans hung on the tip of his tongue, but he managed to change the word before it slipped out.

"People," he said.

She grinned like she knew exactly what he meant. Then she caught sight of the book on his bedside table and crooked an eyebrow. *"Pride and Prejudice?"*

He shrugged. "I might have. . . leafed through a little bit."

She smiled. "Oh yes?"

He swallowed away his reticence. "Yep. I was wondering about Darcy. I don't get it."

Down at the bottom of the stairs, the dog looked up.

Sophie tilted her head. "Don't get what?"

"Why you named your dog after the guy. He was a jerk to her. At least at first."

Sophie shook her head. "I like Mr. Darcy because he's honest and he doesn't care about money. Because Elizabeth changes him, and he becomes a better man."

Chase mulled that one over for a minute. That fit the dog, he supposed.

Fits us too, his wolf pointed out.

Luckily, Sophie dropped the subject and picked up another book, chuckling. *"The Do It Yourself Guide to Biodiesel and Alternative Fuels?* You have a wide range of tastes."

He smiled. "I guess I do."

He reached past her to straighten an uneven row of books then bit his lip. The motion had brought them even closer, and damn, did she smell good.

Judging by the way her breath hitched. Sophie noticed him too. She didn't move away, though. In fact, she shifted her weight to let their sides brush.

Outside, a bird sang cheerily, and down in the kitchen, a sheet of paper fluttered in the breeze of the overhead fan.

"Do you have a favorite?" she whispered.

Chase had a hard time processing words, the way his wolf was going wild inside. If she stepped any closer...

Sophie's right foot inched forward, sending him that much closer to the brink.

"Favorite...?" he mumbled. Sophie was his favorite everything. His destined mate. Is that what she meant?

"Favorite book," she said, cupping his cheek. She shifted slightly until he was sure she was lining up for a kiss. A kiss that would take place half a step away from his bed.

You know you want her, his wolf growled.

Hell yes, he did. Something was supposed to be holding him back, but he couldn't remember what it was any more. Hell, he could barely think.

"*Three Musketeers,*" he managed in a hoarse voice. "All for one, and one for all." Though, honestly, pack loyalty had faded into the background at that moment. All he wanted was his mate.

And she wants us, his wolf murmured as Sophie slid her hands over his shoulders.

"That figures." She chuckled, but her eyes were a little glassy — like his, he supposed. Which made sense, because he could barely think straight. Did she feel the same way?

I guarantee she does, his wolf hummed.

Chase wrapped his arms around her waist and pulled her closer, bringing her right up against his chest.

"Sophie," he whispered, wishing he could explain.

She pressed a hand over his lips and looked him straight in the eye. "I want this, Chase. I need this."

He gulped, because even in the haze of his mind, he knew that *this* came with a lot of complications Sophie wasn't fully aware of.

"Chase," she whispered in a voice that cracked with need.

He meant to say something — anything — but he couldn't, because a second later, he was kissing her. She pressed her body against his and opened her mouth under his. For the first few seconds, Chase barely let his lips move. But then the wall he'd constructed to hold back the need, the yearning — Christ, the desire — that had been building up in him started to crack, and the last of his resistance crashed to the ground. His hands slid from her waist to the lower edge of her breasts. Their hips squeezed together, making his cock hard. Sophie's hungry whimpers grew louder, and she plucked at his shirt, making it clear what she wanted. The way she pulled him in was an extension of that *Please hold me* hug she'd initiated before, and he wanted to cover as much of her as he could. To shield her from the outside world. To make her feel good.

Definitely need to make our mate feel good, his wolf said.

"Yes," Sophie breathed, arching into his touch.

Which was about as clear an affirmation as a man could wish for — or even a shifter at his breaking point.

"Sophie," Chase whispered, lowering her to the bed.

Chapter Eleven

Sophie took a deep breath. Not because of what she was about to do, but because being lowered by Chase was like floating through a cloud. How a man that powerful managed to combine *gentle* with *urgent*, she had no clue. But boy, did it work for her.

It was crazy, how badly she wanted him. How much *naughty* there was hiding inside the nice girl she'd always been.

"I want this," she whispered in an echo of her own words.

She'd had a hell of a day, and her nerves were still on edge. But Chase made the fear fade into the background, and the more she touched him, the more her world filled with joy and light. So she fumbled with his shirt until he helped her work it off, and wow — there she was, flat on her back with an acre of smooth, hard chest above her. Her hands went right on smoothing circles across his skin, unable to get enough of him. How was it possible that they hadn't gone this far before?

Not far enough, a needy part of her body yowled. *Not yet, it isn't.*

She panted for air between kisses and worked her hands down his torso, not sure whether to laugh or curse herself for not getting to this point sooner with him. She'd only had sex twice, and neither time had lived up to the hype. What a fool she'd been for thinking that it would be the same with Chase. She was already halfway to an orgasm, and he hadn't even gotten her naked yet. How amazing would it be to feel Chase's hands in more intimate places?

Still, if it had been about sex and nothing else, she might have shied away. But with Chase, there wasn't just the raw, physical need, but love and trust too.

The locket warmed on her chest and, wow. If that was a reflection of how hot her body was, Chase had better watch out.

He stopped kissing and pulled back, studying her as if to see whether she was okay with more.

"Yes," she assured him, pushing her hips upward until they ground against his groin. *Give me more. Please.*

It was funny, what passion could do to a girl's mind, because she could have sworn his hazel eyes started to glow.

Chase swooped down, covering her lips until she was whimpering for more. Then he inched lower, sucking her lower lip... tickling her chin... kissing her neck. When he scraped his teeth across the soft skin, she arched back, silently begging for more. But a moment later, Chase drew away with a gasp, as if he had suddenly thrown on the brakes.

Her neck tingled, and part of her wished he would have bitten her. Just a little nip. That would be fun.

But Chase seemed intent on avoiding that at all costs. Instead, he nuzzled her, and she hummed, relishing the slight burn of his stubble. If his touch felt that good against her neck, how good would it feel when he got a little lower and—

"Oh," she squeaked when he moved down to her breast. His hand swept up at the same time, pushing her shirt and bra aside. Then his lips touched down on her bare skin, and she moaned.

"Okay?" he whispered out of the side of his mouth.

God, yes, she wanted to say. She wove her fingers through his hair instead, holding him close. *Okay* was the understatement of the year, especially once his soft lips homed in on her nipple and finally captured it. She bucked up under him, writhing and moaning.

"So good... "

Chase didn't say a word, though his eyes flashed, telling her he was just as blown away by the experience as she was, and he couldn't wait for more. At the same time, that shy, puppy-dog vulnerability was still there, making her melt. This wasn't a man out to add a notch to his bedpost. More like a man-child — quiet and sensitive, yet powerful and even wise.

Looking into his eyes was like looking into the soulful eyes of a dog hoping for a new home.

She nearly laughed at that one. If anything, she was the stray brought in from the cold.

"Hang on," she managed, helping him work her shirt and bra off. Then she sank back again. Chase followed, never more than an inch from her body.

"So beautiful," he murmured before getting to work on her right breast.

Stars shot off in her mind as he kissed and suckled. Gently then harder, until she was sure she would explode. At first, she lay still, a willing prisoner to his touch. But gradually, without even being aware of it, she did more than just wait for his attention. She brought the soft flesh of her breast toward his mouth. One hand strayed lower, and she found herself palming the bulge in his jeans. The moment she realized it, her eyes flew open. Chase's, on the other hand, drooped to half-mast. He dipped his hips to grind against the pressure she applied. And when he stopped kissing her, it was just long enough to pop open the button of his jeans.

Is that all right? his eyes asked.

Sophie nodded quickly. It scared her, just how right it felt. How badly she wanted to stroke every inch of his hot, hard flesh.

Which she got to spend the next minutes doing. Delighting in, as a matter of fact. Feeling incredibly naughty but oh-so-good at the same time. She barely remembered how she managed to work her own shorts down along the way. But there she was, naked but for her underwear, wrapped around the man of her dreams.

The barn was quiet — too quiet, considering the dogs were downstairs. Were they listening? She decided it didn't matter. All that mattered was Chase quenching the inferno blazing deep in her core.

Yes, she nearly moaned when Chase slid a hand down her belly.

He paused at the waistband of her panties, and she moaned again.

Yes. Please. More.

She was fairly sure she hadn't said that aloud, but Chase was so tuned in to her, he kept moving after that briefest hesitation, dragging her panties down. Pushing them past her knees and finally her ankles. When she kicked the panties off, he placed his hand on her inner thigh and inched slowly upward, giving her plenty of time to gasp or protest.

In the end, it was her, spreading her legs, giving him space, silently begging for more. Not begging for long, though, because the moment Chase sensed her wordless *Okay*, he rushed to satisfy her.

She gasped — not in surprise but in sheer pleasure. And when Chase dipped his head, rolling his lips around her nipple while exploring her most intimate spot, she arched right off the bed.

"Yes. . . "

Chase dragged the flat of his hand between her legs, making her rock. Then he dipped a finger into her, inching deeper then circling around.

Yes, she wanted to scream. *Yes, yes, yes.* Not just at that specific sensation — she meant everything. Sometimes, it took real searching to find the beauty in life. But at times like this, when her heart filled to bursting and her blood rushed, the world seemed infused with goodness and love.

Love. She barely managed to bite the word back. Surely, it was too soon to go that far?

Not too soon, a little voice said. *You've waited long enough.*

And just like that, her need ratcheted up another notch, and she went back to stroking Chase's cock. Locking eyes with her lover until their movements mirrored each other. He pushed while she tugged, and they both started rocking as if already joined in the world's most primal dance.

"Chase," she panted, lifting her head off the pillow.

When he glanced up, the look in his eyes nearly bowled her over. The need. The animal intensity.

Yes? his arched eyebrows asked.

She signaled toward the bedside table. "Condom. Please. I need you inside."

His eyes flickered, and when he reached hesitantly into the bedside table, she had the sinking suspicion he might not have one. But then his face lit up, and he pulled out a strip of condoms. Had he forgotten he'd had some in there?

Sophie didn't care. She was a cat in heat, and boy, did she need him badly.

She helped him slip a condom out of the wrapper — and even helped him unroll it over his straining cock, much to her own shock. She'd never been that forward before.

Before wasn't with Chase, her subconscious pointed out.

And damn, was that the truth. No other man had ever pinned her with such a hungry, intense look. A look that promised he would make her howl in pleasure while worshiping her at the same time. Neither had moved so deliberately into position above her, nor looked at her like she was his sole concern.

"Yes," she breathed, hooking her legs around his waist.

"Sophie," he whispered, almost trembling with need.

She gave a curt nod, hoping he sensed how good she felt, how ready she was. He must have, because a moment later, he drew carefully back and thrust deep.

"Yes," she cried, clutching his shoulders.

Chase's lips curled back, and his eyes closed. Did he feel the same achy, delicious burn she did? Was his pulse racing as much as hers?

His Adam's apple bobbed, and he resettled his weight, then repeated the move. Faster. Harder. Hungrier. Slowly, he slid out of her, only to hammer back in.

"Yes," she moaned. She didn't need gentle. She needed hot and hard.

Yes, her. The good girl. The quiet one. The one who kept so much locked up inside. She had her needs too, and they'd been pent up for too long.

"Yes," she said, more demanding than ever.

Chase hitched her right leg higher against his body and thrust again. She howled, because the angle intensified the exquisite pleasure. Her ears pounded with her pulse, and something gleamed on her chest — her sweat, intermingled with the shine of his. When she inhaled, she caught their own sensual scent. A thick, sweet aroma that made her head go light.

Chase took her hands and pinned them above her head. That anchored her in place — a damn good thing, because she was starting to move up the mattress with each of his thrusts.

Sophie opened and closed her eyes, caught between two worlds. On the face of it, sex was raw and gritty. Almost dirty. But all she sensed was magic. That and a nearly insatiable desire. She almost wailed, because as high as each of Chase's hard pumps made her, her body always demanded more. Ultimate, indescribable pleasure was within her grasp, yet somehow too far.

"Soon," Chase murmured in a hoarse whisper. "Soon, my love."

She exhaled, forcing herself to relax. To move with him and let the pleasure build naturally instead of forcing it. Seconds must have ticked by before his words clicked. Love?

A warm rush flooded her body, and Chase smiled at her. A smile like a beam of light, making her sure *love* was exactly right. Then he went all serious again and drew back.

"Hey," she protested.

He shook his head, begging her to understand. "Like this. Okay?"

Her eyes went wide as he maneuvered her legs over his shoulders until they were firmly hooked in place. Oh God. Was he going to—

"Oh," she moaned, stretching the sound out over several syllables when he powered back in. The angle was just right, and her need reached a new peak. All the heat in her body pulled back like a wave getting ready to break.

Chase held her tight, and she met his push with an inner squeeze that made them both gasp. Their separate strokes became a steady rhythm that would have made any normal bed rock. A good thing the mattress was on the floor — and not just for that reason. She already felt high, lying in that airy loft — not to mention the feeling of an intense orgasm building inside.

Her hands fisted the sheets as the heat between their bodies intensified.

Yes... Yes... She started chanting — possibly out loud, or maybe just in her head.

Chase pumped faster, plunging deeper, until—

She howled, clenching down with all the power she had. Then she shuddered, and a thousand shooting stars exploded in her mind.

"Yes!"

The dam inside her burst, making the ache give way to pleasure greater than anything she'd ever felt. A rush of heat. A burst of energy. A feeling of floating above the earth.

Chase's hands tightened until he stiffened, coming a heartbeat after she did. Both remained perfectly still, forming a living, breathing statue of two lovers at the peak of pleasure. Sophie looked over herself, preserving the erotic vision in her mind. She took in her body, wrapped around Chase's. The line of muscle running down the center of Chase's abdomen, all the way down to where they were joined.

She bit her lip. Chase was inside her. She could feel the throbbing heat, the pulsing energy. And beyond that, she felt a spiritual connection that was totally unique.

Yes, an earthy voice whispered. *You are connected. He is yours, and you are his.*

She sank into the mattress, too overcome to process what that voice might have been. Destiny, or a whole lot of hormones that might make her think that about anyone?

Not just anyone, she decided, rejecting the thought immediately. *Only Chase.*

Then it hit her that her legs were still hooked over his shoulders, and the utter bliss of her orgasm gave way to self-consciousness. Oh Lord. She looked like someone on one of those naughty Greek vases museums didn't put in the front of their showcases.

For a moment, her insecurities threatened to sneak back in, but when Chase scrubbed his chin against the inside of her leg with a look of utter rapture, her doubts vanished. She felt good, damn it. Better than ever. Why feel shy about that?

She giggled, making Chase look up, wearing that expression she loved.

You're so funny, his eyes seemed to say. *I may not understand you, but I love everything about you.*

"What?" he murmured, hitting a deep, gravelly tone. A sound of pure male satisfaction.

"That tickles." She laughed. "But I like it."

A grin spread on his face — gradually, like dawn, and just as bright, just as mysterious. "I like it too."

He scrubbed a little more, then released her slowly until they were lying side by side. The ceiling fan turned quietly overhead, cooling her skin. Outside, crickets chirped and trees swayed in the sea breeze. Chase rolled away, disposing of the condom, then hurried back to her and drew her into a tight embrace. Face-to-face, chest-to-chest, with the locket pressed between them.

"Feels so good," she couldn't help sighing. "But there's just one thing."

He tensed as if alarmed not to have met her every need. "What?"

She stroked his cheek and nestled closer. "Why didn't we do that earlier?"

At first, his expression was blank, but then they both cracked into laughter at the same time.

"Funny," Chase murmured, hugging her tightly. "I was wondering the same thing."

Chapter Twelve

Chase wrapped his arms around Sophie and held her close. Really close, the way you did with a dream you didn't want to slip away. There was so much he wanted to tell her — and so much he wanted to hear her say. At the same time, he relished the sweet silence. He had his mate. What more did he need?

Still, he was acutely aware that sooner or later, those words would have to come. Sophie was right about having waited too long to have slept together. Had he waited too long to tell her about his inner wolf, too?

"Sophie," he whispered, gathering his courage to spill it all at last.

She smiled the sweet, hazy smile of a person who'd never felt so satisfied. "Yes?"

God, he loved her. Should he start with that?

He kissed her shoulder, then her collarbone, and finally the upper part of her breast. Partly to buy time, and partly because he finally could. All those gorgeous curves, all that smooth flesh open for him to explore. . .

Her locket rested between her breasts, and her eyes shone as she looked down. He rested his chin on her chest and looked up at her. That was a whole new perspective he could spend hours growing familiar with. Her long, dark locks spread over the pillow, curling this way and that, and he wrapped his finger in one.

"Always wanted to do that," he admitted.

Sophie bit her lip. "Me too. I mean, for you to do that."

Gently, he combed his fingers along one long lock of her hair until it lay along her chest instead of over the sheets. Which wasn't the best idea when it came to spilling the truth, because that led his gaze over the rest of her body, distracting him all over again.

Talk later. Love now, his wolf mumbled from its lazy, post-coital doze.

And just like that, he replayed it all in his mind. The ecstasy. The intensity — so much, he'd even imagined some mystical force powering both of them. The shattering high, and the incredible afterglow.

Again, his wolf begged. *Let's do it again.*

Tempting as that was, he shook the thought away. He had to talk to Sophie. The sun had long since set, and the moon was rising outside — a fitting backdrop to what he had to tell her. But Sophie started speaking before he could, and he couldn't bear to stop her.

"I feel like I've known you forever, you know that?" she whispered, touching his cheek.

That's destiny, he wanted to say.

"As if I was saving myself for you, even way back when I lived in Maine and Vermont..."

"Vermont?"

She nodded. "Friends of friends had a farm there, and they gave me a job." Her smile grew. "They had a little of everything. Vegetables, flowers, even alpacas."

He laughed. "Alpacas?"

She nodded. "I loved it there. I had a greenhouse all to myself." Her eyes strayed to the window, and she laughed outright. "Kind of the opposite of Maui. Not much need for greenhouses here, huh?"

He chuckled. Yeah, it was different from where he'd grown up, too. He sniffed deeply, wondering what destiny had in store for him. A nice, quiet life in Maui with Sophie, or the life of a vagabond wolf out in the wild?

He held her hands tightly, as if destiny might sneak up and steal Sophie away.

"If you could do anything, what would it be?" he whispered.

Sophie smiled shyly. "Honestly, I like my life now. I like working at the smoothie truck, and I love Maui. I love..." Her voice hitched, and for the span of a heartbeat, Chase thought she might finish with *you. I love you.* But instead, she rushed on. "Seeing you. I love being able to see you every day."

"I love that too," he murmured, holding her hands close to his heart.

For the next few seconds, they got stuck there, gazing into each other's eyes.

I love you, Chase practiced in his mind. *I love you.* Why was it so hard to say?

Maybe because the word was overused. He'd heard humans say it a thousand times, and they weren't always sincere. Still, he meant it. *I love you, Sophie. More than I can say.*

But all he actually got out was, "That's all you want?"

Sophie burst out laughing and play-smacked his arm. "That happens to be enough for me, mister. Well, okay," she admitted. "I wouldn't mind having a vegetable garden."

Chase grinned and stroked her cheek with his thumb. Some women dreamed of diamonds and fame. Sophie wanted a garden.

Hell, I'll dig her one, his wolf declared. *Best damn garden in the world. Right here.*

"Don't forget about books," he added.

Her eyes drifted over the bookshelves, and Chase wondered if she was picturing herself living there. Or was that wishful thinking on his part?

Sophie nodded. "Lots and lots of books, and time to read them." Then she wiggled a little in his arms and looked into his eyes. "What about you? If you could do anything, what would it be?"

Mate with you, his wolf said immediately.

"I guess I'd get myself a job in Lahaina and buy myself a smoothie every day."

Her smile stretched. "You like those smoothies, huh?"

He shook his head. "No. I mean, yes. But mainly, I like you." Then he shook his head. "I more than like you, Sophie." His mouth went dry, but he went on anyway. If not now, then when? "Sophie, I love y—"

She pressed a finger to his lips and closed her eyes. "I want to hear you say that," she whispered, looking more wistful than he'd ever seen her. "More than anything. But I think..." She trailed off, cleared her throat, and started again. "I think I ought to tell you everything about me first. Just in case."

He hated the doubt in her voice. Nothing in the world would shake his love for her. Didn't she know that?

On the other hand, he could relate all too well. He needed to tell Sophie about his shifter side. So he took a deep breath and opened his mouth to insist he speak first. But a soft knock sounded below, and the dogs started barking hysterically. Darcy threw himself at the door, and Sophie sat up, clutching the sheet to her chest.

"Coco! Darcy! Boris! Quiet!" she called.

Chase sighed. It wasn't the dogs' fault. It was Connor's for coming by. What could his brother possibly want at a time like this?

Getting out of bed had never been such torture, because Sophie was there, and he didn't want to leave. But he stood reluctantly and pulled on his pants. "I'll be right back."

Sophie nodded, looking just as mournful as he felt. It was a good thing the mattress was close to the edge of the loft, and that the stairs were so steep. The only way to descend them was facing in, like a ladder. When he got to the third step down, he paused to kiss her.

"Nice," she murmured.

He grinned. "Really nice. I'll be right back, okay?"

She nodded, and down he went, placing his feet carefully. The dogs were milling around the bottom stairs, barking to alert him to the intruder at the door as if he hadn't noticed anything.

"Good dog," he murmured, leaning over to pet whichever dog got under his hands first.

It was crazy, how excited the dogs were, as if they'd already accepted this as home and had to defend it at all costs. And just as crazy was how normal it all felt to him — having Sophie in his bed and the dogs in his house. Like they were already one big, happy family that had been living together for years.

Catching the thought before his wolf ran away with it, he stepped to the door.

"All right already," he ordered. "Settle down."

They obeyed — even Darcy, although that took a pointed stare to achieve — and Chase swung the door open to greet Connor.

"Uh, hi," his brother said, standing three feet back from the threshold. Yeah, Connor knew he had crappy timing, all right.

Chase stepped outside with a grimace and closed the door as soon as the dogs squeezed out. They all rushed forward and sniffed Connor's feet.

Connor cursed, stepping back. "You working on forming your own pack?" Then he scowled at Darcy, who stood by the front door, snarling. *Cut that out, or I'll turn you into a hot dog.*

Darcy looked at Chase, alarmed.

Chase nodded to the little spitfire. *Dragon shifter. Watch out.*

The poor dog looked a little shaken, but he stood his ground, letting the world know he'd defend his mistress to his dying breath.

"Tough little guy, aren't you?" Connor grinned. The expression faded as soon as he got down to business, though. "Look, sorry to bother you."

Chase didn't bother masking his displeasure. Connor might be the oldest brother and leader of their pack, but this was Chase's house, and that was his mate inside. His mussed hair and bare chest were a dead giveaway at what he and Sophie had been up to, but he ignored Connor's knowing look.

"What is it?"

"Just a heads-up." Connor glanced up at an open window, then pulled Chase far enough away for the sound of distant surf to cover their voices. "We just got word that Moira is on the move."

The wind whipped around Chase's legs, making his blood run cold. Moira, the ruthless she-dragon with a vendetta against the shifters of Koa Point?

"What is she up to now?"

Connor ran a hand through his hair. "All we know is that several of her mercenaries are booked on a flight to Oahu."

Chase looked back toward the barn, and while he couldn't see Sophie, he could sense her there, and his body yearned to return to her side.

Hold her, his wolf growled. *Protect her, and never, ever leave.*

Chase sighed. If only the world could be the sunny place Sophie tried so hard to believe in.

"Is it the dragon slayer we keep hearing rumors about?" he asked.

Connor frowned deeply, looking a decade older than his usual self. "Could be, could be not. Maybe just another shifter. We hope it's a false alarm but..."

Chase grimaced. Hope only took a man so far. The rest was all legwork. But, damn. He looked at his brother, resigned. "What do you need me to do?"

Connor clapped him on the shoulder in an *Attaboy* gesture. "Right now, nothing. Jenna and I are flying to Oahu to keep an eye out for Moira's men. Meanwhile, the others will keep investigating our leads. You have the night, at least." Connor's eyes wandered back to the house. "But fair warning — you need to be ready to move in the morning if we need you."

Chase nodded grimly. They'd left the military, but some things never changed, especially in the dark and dangerous shifter world.

Connor studied him closely then leaned in to whisper, "There is one more thing."

Chase squinted at his brother, waiting for whatever bombshell his brother was about to drop.

"About Sophie," Connor said. "I know you didn't want us investigating her, but this just came back from the police. Her last name isn't Wilkins. It's Brenner. Did you know that?"

Chase's inner wolf growled. *Who cares about Sophie's name? We know our mate.*

He shook his head at Connor, refusing to take the bait. "So what? Maybe she wants her privacy. Maybe she's on the run."

"Maybe she's hiding," Connor added with a hard look.

"What, like Jenna was when she came here?" Chase shot back, feeling his cheeks flush.

Connor put his hands up. "Look, I'm not judging her. But it is something you need to be aware of."

Oh, Chase was *aware* of a lot of things — like how tempted he was to punch Connor. What right did his brother have, digging into Sophie's business?

"All I'm saying is some things are not as they seem. Maybe you two need to have a little talk," Connor said.

Chase gritted his teeth. He had been getting around to that when Connor had come along. Damn the man!

Then he caught himself. His brother was only trying to help. "What about the bullet we dug out of the wall of the truck?" he asked, trying to keep cool.

"Looks like it was fired from a Steyr, but that's all we've got."

Chase frowned. Steyrs were renowned sniper rifles — and someone had aimed one at Sophie?

"What have you found on this guy David?" he demanded.

"We're working on that," Connor said. "They really did grow up in the same place, and they really did go their separate ways. We're still trying to uncover what David has been up to recently. But, Chase. Let me just warn you. Sophie's got one hell of a wacky family."

Chase made a face. "What, like ours?"

Connor laughed outright and smacked him on the shoulder. "You got that right, baby brother." Then he jerked his chin in the direction of the house. "Listen, I won't keep you. You've got tonight. But come morning. . ." His voice dropped in warning.

Chase heaved a heavy breath. Duty called — again. Well, he'd answer, as he always did. In the meantime, he had time to devote to his mate.

He nodded slowly. "Tell the others to get me as soon as they have something."

But not a second earlier, his wolf snarled.

Connor stood still, having said all he'd intended to, but not quite ready to go. Chase wasn't ready to either. For all that he yearned to get back to Sophie, he had his brother to think of. In a worst-case scenario, Connor and Jenna could be flying into an all-out dragon fight.

Chase shuffled in place then finally spoke. "You take care, man. Watch your back."

That reminded him of the army, too. The little goodbyes. The huge, unspoken fears. How often had *It's probably nothing* become famous last words?

Connor flashed a cocky smile. "That's supposed to be my line."

That was just like the army, too. The bravado. The *Don't worry, I'll be okay.*

Chase started to clap his brother on the arm, but it turned into a hug. Just a quick one, just in case. Connor's powerful arms squeezed as tightly as a boa before releasing him.

"Yikes. I smell sex." Connor shooed him back toward the barn with a broad grin. "Get back to your mate where you belong."

Chase couldn't help smiling. His mate. God, he loved the sound of that.

Connor lumbered down the path, but Chase called out from the front door. "Hey."

Connor turned with an expectant look.

"Tell the guys — and the girls — thanks. For everything."

Connor grinned. "The throw pillows weren't my idea." Then he added in a mental aside, *But the condoms. . .*

Chase cleared his throat and made a show of herding the dogs back into the house. Sometimes, his brothers drove him crazy. Other times, he could just about kiss them. Most of the time, it was a mix of both.

He smiled. One crazy family.

The thought chased his smile away, replacing it with a frown. What had Connor said about Sophie?

A cloud slipped over the moon — one of many, he noted. A sign of change in the air. He stepped inside, brow furrowed in consternation. Sophie had come to the bottom of the stairs, waiting for him, and he couldn't help brightening again.

"Is everything okay?" she asked, looking concerned.

More than okay, his wolf growled. Sophie was wearing the shirt he'd discarded not too long ago — and not much else. He breathed deeply, loving how their scents had mingled.

He stepped over for a hug. A hell of a hug, as it turned out, because the shyness between them was gone. Well, mostly gone. Sophie blushed as she always did, and his face heated too. Now he knew why his brothers and Dell always looked so dopey around their mates. They were absolutely, totally, hopelessly in love. Just like him.

"I might have to check on some things in the morning," he said, resting his cheek against her silky hair. "But we're good for tonight."

"No sign of the shooter?" Her voice wavered, and her grip on his shoulders tightened.

"They're following a few leads, but nothing right now." Chase let a couple of heartbeats tick by, wondering if he should get to that talk now. But he was still too edgy after Connor's warnings, and his wolf was pacing inside. "Do you want a bite?"

He meant the food basket, but his wolf shot back a lusty, *Yes. A mating bite.*

"Sure," Sophie said, sounding glad for the distraction.

Together, they picked through the offerings — fancy bread, cheese, and ham — and ate at the kitchen counter. The dogs sat in an orderly row, making a show of how well-behaved they could be in hope of some morsels. Chase was torn between shooing them all away, tough alpha style, and showing a little heart. Those mutts had been Sophie's sole comfort before he'd come along, and they'd saved her life. He owed them forever for that.

He flipped a tiny piece of sausage to Darcy. *For taking good care of my mate.*

You mean, my nice lady, the little dog huffed back.

Chase let that one slide. There was enough conflict in the world. No need to add more.

"Oh, look." Sophie pulled a container out of the basket. "Strawberries. Yum."

Chase smiled. Back in the army, guys tried to help each other forget the perils of the outside world, but it was hard. Sophie could make his mind go blissfully blank with a few words.

She held out a strawberry, and he ate it from her hand. So much for being a tough alpha.

"Good, huh?" She laughed.

He closed his eyes, masking his expression. Oh, it was good, all right. Not just for the berry flavor, but as a reminder of how he'd gotten to brush his lips over her body a short time ago. Her mouth. . . her neck. . . her nipples. . .

He shifted sideways to give his hardening cock more space.

"Want another one?" she asked.

He risked a glance in her direction. Was that a tease in her voice?

Sophie's eyes were merry, her cheeks bright red. Oh, she was teasing, all right.

"Sure." His voice was husky as hell, the way it got after he shifted out of wolf form.

Sophie held out another berry and gripped the stem while he bit down.

Definitely teasing. His wolf licked its lips.

He kept his gaze locked on Sophie the whole time, trying to keep the glow of lust out of his eyes. A losing battle because, damn. His cock was rock hard, his pulse all over the place. Before long, he had Sophie boxed in against the kitchen counter and his lips against her ear.

"You want more space?" he whispered, desperately hoping she'd say no.

She slid her hands down his ass. "I want less space."

A zing of excitement rushed through his veins.

"How's this?" He hoisted her onto the kitchen counter and stepped into the vee between her knees.

"Perfect," she breathed. Her fingers splayed across his belly, and her thumb toyed with his navel.

116

He bit his lip then reached behind her and pushed everything aside — the food basket, the toaster, everything. The salt and pepper shakers toppled off the far end of the counter, making the dogs scatter.

"Chase!" Sophie admonished, but there was a gleam in her eye.

"Sophie," he growled, covering her mouth with his.

That kiss was hotter and hungrier than ever before, and he nestled closer, letting her feel just how hard he was.

"How's this?" he whispered, dragging his lips along her neck.

A tiny moan escaped her lips, and she tilted her head back. "Even better."

He would have chuckled, but he was too busy. All that hair, all that smooth skin. Where to begin?

His wolf gave a little huff. *Isn't it obvious?*

He moved slowly, sliding his hands up her thighs one delicious inch at a time, rolling away the edge of the T-shirt that barely covered her.

The room was quiet, the dogs having retreated to a far corner of the barn. Sophie sighed deeply and spread her legs wider, inviting him in.

"I have a new answer," she murmured, tilting her head back.

He glanced up. "To what?"

She gasped as his thumb touched down between her legs. Then she swallowed a few times and spoke in a shaky voice. "If I could do anything, I would do this. Exactly this." She threaded her fingers through his hair and rocked against his hand.

Chase raked his teeth against her neck then took a deep breath. So many options. So many rewards. But if he took things too fast, would Sophie shy away?

"More," she protested when he paused.

His wolf goaded him on. *She'll like it. I swear she will.*

And fool that he was, Chase listened. He pulled her shirt a little higher and backed away from the counter without letting his lips leave her body. He dipped lower and lower, gripping her thighs, praying she wouldn't stop him.

"Nice," she whispered.

When he kissed the top of her thigh, Sophie guided his head to her center. She leaned back to give him more space, holding her breath.

He came down over her core gently, but as soon as her sweet flavor registered on his tongue...

"Oh, yes..." she moaned, holding him close.

He licked hard and deep, like the wild wolf he was.

He held back her soft flesh with his thumbs, determined to make her come as hard and as fast as possible. And all that time, Sophie whimpered under his tongue.

Yes, his wolf growled. *Make our mate come...*

A moment later, Sophie cried out. Every muscle in her body bunched, and he held her, still lapping away.

"So good..." she murmured, going limp in his arms.

He held her, and at first, it was like holding a rag doll. Gradually, Sophie straightened, and her eyes focused. He'd never seen her look so calm. Loving. Serene.

Then the color rose in her cheeks, and her eyes shone brighter.

"That was good for me. But poor you," she cooed, sliding a seductive finger over his cock.

"Yeah, poor me." Chase groaned. "The condoms are all the way up there." He drooped over her shoulder as his cock ached.

Sophie cleared her throat primly. "Most of the condoms are up there. But if you look closely..."

He looked up as she patted the breast pocket of the shirt. The woman was a genius.

She guided his hand to her breast until all that soft goodness warmed his palm. And in the middle... He reached in and plucked out a foil packet.

"Good thing someone was thinking." Sophie fluttered her eyelashes.

He ripped the packet open then paused, offering it to her. She didn't take the condom, but she kept her hands over his while he put it on.

"And what exactly were you thinking?" he asked, barely breathing.

She pulled the shirt over her head — slowly, giving him time to drink his fill. Then she wrapped her legs around his waist and her arms around his shoulders, drawing him closer. Her nipples brushed his chest, and her silky hair tickled his collarbone. As if that weren't enough, she caressed his ears, driving his inner wolf wild.

"I was thinking you deserve some fun too," she whispered.

Chase worked his jaw back and forth a few times. *Fun* wasn't the right word, not for all the emotions welling up in his chest, nor for the sheer physical need his body quivered with. But words weren't his thing. Deeds were.

He cupped both sides of her ass and drew her toward him, gritting his teeth while she took in his straining cock. Slowly, drawing out that glorious burn.

She gasped into his ear. "Deeper."

Her words were more command than dirty talk, and he pushed forward, suppressing a groan. She was so slick, so snug around him. Tight but yielding at the same time. He withdrew then pushed back in, making her cry out.

"Oh!"

His eyes narrowed to slits, but he kept them locked on her face, watching as her expression changed. Concentrated at first, then more rapturous. Before long, they were both panting, clutching, moaning. . .

Sophie, he wanted to howl. *You are my mate. My one and only.*

His canines ached, desperate to extend, but that was the only thing he held back. The need to pleasure her had free rein. The instinct to mark her with his scent. The urgent need to fill his woman, again and again. . .

Her body tensed — a signal that she was about to come, and he timed his hardest thrust for them to both come at the same time.

"Yes. . ." she moaned, clenching around him

Yes, his wolf hissed as he released deep inside her body.

Adrenaline blazed through his body, and he stood still as a statue, hanging on to every drop of his bliss. When Sophie cried out in an aftershock, he drove into her one more time, making her moan. And when she slumped in his arms, he forced his stiff limbs to loosen and cradle her. His chest rose and fell with every short breath. Sophie held him tightly, chin tucked over his shoulder, fingers splayed over his back. One warm tear rolled down his skin, followed by another, and he pulled away. Oh God. Had he been too rough? Too fast? Too deep?

Sophie dragged a hand across her eyes and smiled. "I'm sorry. I'm good." She buried her head against his shoulder. "I'm more than good. In so many ways. . ."

He wrapped his arms around her so far they overlapped. Then he nestled up against her ear. "I know what you mean."

"Do you? Because I've never, ever felt this good." She rocked in his arms.

Chase inhaled their intermingled scents and felt pure contentment heat his bones. "Neither have I," he whispered. "Neither have I."

Chapter Thirteen

Sophie turned slowly, barely opening her eyes before shutting them again. It was morning — she could tell that much — but she was afraid the previous night had been a dream. What if she hadn't just spent the best night of her life wrapped in a perfect man's arms?

But that weight on her leg wasn't one of the dogs cuddled up alongside, and she wasn't imagining the tough, wiry fingers intertwined with hers. Slowly, she opened her eyes. Then she closed them again, exhaling in relief. She really was cuddled up with Chase, and she really had spent the night in that cozy loft with him.

The clock showed shortly past six. Chase was still spooned up behind her, snoozing peacefully. Was he wiped out, or would he awake all energized? She felt a little of both, though she had the sneaking suspicion the *energized* part might take over again and lead them into yet another round of sex.

A huge grin spread on her face as she relived what they'd done in the wee hours of the morning. When she'd stirred at the first hint of daylight, Chase had kissed her shoulder, and before long, they were shagging like bunnies all over again.

Not like bunnies. Like wolves, Chase had corrected her when she'd joked afterward.

Wolf was an apt description, because not only had they gone at it on all fours, they'd done so with a raw, animal intensity she didn't think she was capable of. Even Chase — her sweet, tender lover — had shown his wilder side, nipping her neck and thrusting into her like never before. When they'd collapsed into a heap afterward, huffing and panting, she could have sworn she heard him whisper a single word.

Mine.

She closed her eyes, hugging his arm to her belly. She wanted to be his, and for him to be hers.

"Morning," Chase whispered, bringing her gaze around.

She rolled to look at him, and it hit her all over again — how genuine he was. How sweet.

How built, the naughty part of her mind added after a peek at his chiseled torso.

Still, that hint of vulnerability was there, though she couldn't quite explain why. It was endearing as anything, but it worried her at the same time. What was it that haunted his quiet, introspective soul?

"Morning," she whispered.

"Morning," he echoed.

A second later, they both laughed, because there they were again, all starry-eyed just from being together.

"You make me tongue-tied," she said, pressing her body against his.

"Hmm. Tongue-tied," he murmured, drawing her closer. "I like the sound of that."

They kissed for a good minute then sighed and leaned back, grinning broadly. Her foot bumped Chase's, and after he looked down, he spent a long time dragging his gaze back to her face.

She blushed, not so much from shyness, but at the realization of how comfortable she was with him looking at her. Then she looked around, trying to get her mind onto something other than his body, hers, or how good she felt. Outside the huge, west-facing windows, the sky was overcast, and a blustery wind made the trees bend and sway. It wasn't shaping up to be a typically beautiful Maui day. But that didn't matter, not when she had Chase and a cozy place to shelter in.

"I love what you've done with this barn. It's great."

He looked around slowly. "It is. But I have to admit, it's not usually this nice. My friends fixed it up a little." Then he sighed. "I guess they've been trying to fix *us* up."

She laughed. "Looks like we owe them, then."

Chase nodded with an expression that said, *More than you could ever know.*

"Were you always so close?"

He mulled that one over for a long time before answering. "I guess so. What about you? No brothers to pester you?"

She laughed. "I always wished for some brothers. Sisters. Anyone." The old sadness seeped back into her, but she pushed it away. "I had a dog, though."

He chuckled. "That figures."

"Roscoe. Best dog ever. Oops." She peeked down toward the ground floor where the dogs lay snoozing. "I mean, from my twelve-year-old point of view."

Chase's eyes twinkled. "What did Roscoe do?"

She shrugged, trying to pick out something concrete from her memories. "He listened." *Like you do.*

Chase waited patiently for more, and yes — that was like Roscoe too. Chase even had his head cocked the way Roscoe once did. And Chase's eyes — they were so earnest, so innocent in a way she couldn't explain.

"We had our own book club, Roscoe and I," she confessed. "We read James Herriot and all the Black Stallion books."

Chase broke out in a laugh heartier than she'd ever heard from him before. "How exactly did that work?"

She smiled at the ceiling. Finally, a nice memory of her younger days. Leave it to Chase to help draw the good out from under the bad. "It worked the way tea parties with stuffed animals do. I would read aloud, and Roscoe would listen." Then she caught Chase's dubious look and swatted him with a pillow. "Men. You wouldn't understand. I bet you played soldier as kids."

Chase shook his head, so she guessed again.

"Did you build a tree house out in the woods?"

"More like a den," he said, watching for her reaction.

She nearly laughed, but something about his expression said he wasn't joking.

"Hey," he murmured. His fingers played nervously over hers, and his cheek developed a slight twitch. "There's something I've been meaning to say for a long time. About me, I mean."

And just like that, the lightness was gone from his voice. But Chase was right. They had put off the more serious stuff for too long, and she needed to get things off her chest. "I have to tell you, too. About me. Who I am. Where I come from."

Chase shook his head. "None of that matters, Sophie. I know who you are. But I have to tell you who I am inside."

She smiled. The poor guy had never been good with words. She knew who he was inside — her sweet, soulful Chase.

"Me first," she insisted. "Please. Just hear me out."

Chase pursed his lips, looking genuinely torn. But then he nodded, humoring her.

"Sophie is my real name, but ever since I came to Maui, I've been using a different last name. My legal name is Brenner." She waited, studying his reaction, but Chase just shrugged. "Brenner, as in Carl Brenner. My mother made me take my stepfather's name when they got married."

Still no reaction. Sophie blinked. Chase had mentioned growing up in a remote area, and he had spent the past decade in the military being posted who-knew-where. Had he somehow missed the headlines that had dominated the North American press a few years ago?

"Carl Brenner. The Spirit of Seventy-Sixers. The attack on the Pentagon?"

Chase tilted his head. "Your stepfather tried to break in to the Pentagon?"

Wow. Apparently, Chase really hadn't heard about it.

"He didn't just try. He got as far as the door to the records rooms. Then all hell broke loose." Her voice choked up a little. Seven people had been killed in the ensuing shootout, and it was all her stepfather's fault. "He's serving seven consecutive life sentences."

Chase stroked her shoulder, mulling it over. "You think he didn't deserve that?"

She shook her head immediately. "He should have gotten the death penalty, if you ask me. But that's not the point, Chase. That criminal is my stepfather. I'm related to the

'Militia Madman.'" She made air quotes as visions of the headlines ghosted through her head. "I grew up with all that. The conspiracy theories. The crazy, unfounded suspicions. The plans for Armageddon."

Chase went right on holding her, showing her he didn't care. "So that's what you meant by being prepared. Stocking up. Bad habits being hard to break."

Her gut knotted as she nodded. Yes, yes, and yes. Would Chase hate her for that?

"That's what you meant about seeing the good things in life," he murmured.

She held her breath, awaiting his verdict. So many people judged her by her family. Surely, Chase would be the same?

But he just shrugged, looking at her, totally unfazed. "My father is a total deadbeat. Who cares about that?"

Sophie squeezed her lips together. It was one thing to have a deadbeat dad. It was another thing to have a father like hers. So she tried once again.

"Did you hear what I just said?"

He nodded. Twice.

She stared. "And?"

He shrugged. "That's someone else. It's not you." He scooted closer, erasing the distance she'd unconsciously created between them. "I know you. You're kind. You look out for people. You're one of those rare people who really means it when you say, 'Have a nice day.'"

She stared. Was he really going to let her off the hook that easily? She'd spent years living with guilt. But Chase just dismissed all that in the blink of an eye.

"You rescue dogs. You plant flowers. You're a good person, Sophie."

She wanted to believe that — desperately. But a corner of her mind kept reminding her of her links to the monster who had preached so much hate and caused so much trouble.

Chase hugged her. "My dad's a jerk, too. Doesn't mean I'm one."

His voice was muffled against her hair, but she could hear the stark determination in it.

"You really don't care?" she asked, pulling back to study his face.

"I really don't care. Though I have to say, I'm curious what records he was after. Or shouldn't I ask?"

She grimaced, and he spoke up immediately. "Forget it. It doesn't matter."

But somehow, it mattered to her. If she and Chase were going to get serious, she had to tell him the truth. The whole truth, and nothing but.

Her mouth went dry, and her hands were all jittery, but she plunged ahead. "He was obsessed with the supernatural. He thought the government was developing the ultimate soldier, and he wanted to get ahold of those plans for himself."

Chase stiffened. "What plans?"

She took a deep breath. This was the tricky part. "He believed in shifters. You know, like werewolves and stuff. Crazy, huh?"

Other than the pulse showing at his neck, Chase could have been a statue.

"Maybe not so crazy," he finally murmured.

Sophie's mouth had never felt drier. "It's not," she admitted in a whisper. "I saw one."

Chase's eyes went wide. "A shifter?"

"Just before I left home. My stepfather was in prison, but his brother, Mike, was obsessed with the idea of shifter power. That would make the militia nearly invincible, so he refused to give up on the idea."

"What idea?" Chase asked in a scratchy, uncertain voice.

"To try to find shifters. To learn about them. To become as strong as they are, because then they'd be unbeatable."

Chase paled. Damn. He had to be thinking she was totally insane. Still, now that she'd started, she wasn't going to stop.

"Mike became obsessed with the subject. When he discovered the Pentagon didn't actually have any real intel on shifters, he decided to try a new tack. He went out, searching for natural-born shifters."

Chase looked genuinely alarmed. "But—"

"I know, it all sounds crazy. But the thing is, he succeeded. Mike found a bear shifter, and he even got the bear to bite his arm on the theory that he would gain that shifting ability for himself."

"Is he nuts?" Chase looked genuinely alarmed. Almost like he knew about shifters or something.

Yes, she wanted to say. *He was.*

She sighed. "Mike believed it. You know, like the old stories. Being bitten by a werewolf and all that."

She'd never seen Chase look more incredulous. "It's not that easy."

She looked off into the distance. "As a kid, I heard the stories. I even thought it would be cool to be a shifter. You know, to change into an animal and sniff around on four feet."

At that point, Chase's expression changed to hopeful, and she wondered why.

"But then I saw it with my own eyes — a man changing into an animal." She swallowed hard. "Mike, I mean. It all happened over a week. He started acting strangely, like he was hearing voices in his head. Then he started changing — getting hairy, then going normal again. He'd scream and bend over, and his legs started changing shape. It was horrible."

Chase whispered so faintly, she barely caught what he said. "Horrible?"

She closed her eyes, fighting away memories. "He was in agony. For two days, that kept happening — he'd shift part-way, then shift back. I saw it with my own eyes. He changed into a bear — or came close. The whole time, he was moaning, like something was eating him from the inside."

It was strange, how the story didn't seem to surprise Chase. But she was so caught up in it, she probably wasn't reading him right.

"It was monstrous. Unnatural. Like nature gone wrong."

Other than going totally white, Chase's face was expressionless. "Unnatural?"

She bobbed her head up and down, wishing she'd never brought up the subject. She puffed out a breath to steady herself and tried to sum things up.

"Mike died a horrible death. My stepfather is in jail — all because they wanted to be shifters. David's father took leadership of the group—"

Chase's chin snapped up. "David?"

She nodded. "At least his father showed more sense than Mike and my stepfather. He forbade anyone from continuing the shifter project, and for a while, things settled down. I'd had enough of it all by then, so I moved to Vermont."

"What about David?" Chase asked, furrowing his brow.

She frowned. "I'm not sure. I haven't seen him in years. Why?"

Chase stared off into the distance, thinking. A full minute later, he murmured, "Just wondering, I guess."

Sophie looked through the windows on the west end of the barn. The weather was blustery and cloudy, much like her mood. Had she ruined everything with Chase?

"I'm sorry," she whispered, taking his hands. "I just had to tell you. I need you to know where I come from. What I left behind and why."

Chase nodded slowly, but he didn't say a word. He didn't even meet her eyes.

She gulped. "I hope that doesn't change anything."

Please, please, please, she wanted to say. *Please don't make me lose you over all that.*

Chase flashed a short, forced smile. His eyes were dull and listless, but his hands were tight on hers, almost as if there was someone out there, ready to yank her away. Mixed messages, in other words. But the words he uttered next just about knocked her out.

"Nothing will change how much I love you."

It was just a whisper, but her jaw dropped. "You... love me?"

His smile was equal parts sweet and sad, and she couldn't understand why. "I've loved you from the start. I love you more than I can say."

As beautiful as his words were, something made her feel there was a *but* coming.

"Your past doesn't matter," Chase went on. "You left that life behind for a reason."

Then... what? she wanted to scream. *Why are we not dancing for joy right now?*

"But something is holding you back," she said, almost choking over the words.

He squeezed her hands. "I don't mind about your family. The problem is my family."

She looked up, aching at the hurt in his voice. "Your family is great. And anyway, it doesn't matter. Nothing will change how much I love you."

His eyes brightened then faded again. "So, I guess it's my turn to tell you. About me, I mean."

She nodded eagerly. Whatever it was, it wouldn't matter. The sooner Chase told her, the sooner she could assure him everything was fine.

"So tell me," she whispered. "Please."

Chapter Fourteen

A heavy silence stretched between them, and Sophie waited impatiently for Chase to begin. Finally, he opened his mouth, ready to start, but then—

His chin jerked up and to the side, as if he'd heard a phone ring. His forehead creased with deep lines, and his whole demeanor changed.

"Damn it," he muttered.

Sophie blinked. "Everything okay?"

His shoulders drooped for a second, and his hands balled into fists. "Yes. No. Shit. I have to go check."

He looked at her for a long, hard minute, and she could see him warring with himself. He stood, reaching for his clothes, then took her hand.

"I'll explain everything, Sophie. I swear."

He kissed her. She wanted to kiss him back, but her lips met thin air as Chase pulled away.

"I swear, I will," he muttered, pulling on his pants.

She'd seen him turn on soldier mode before, but never as abruptly as this. His voice was tight with determination, and his grim undertone scared her. What exactly was going on?

One of his brothers had come by the previous evening, and Chase had come back in, looking preoccupied. *I might have to check on some things in the morning...*

She looked around. What exactly had flipped that switch in him?

Chase was already swinging a foot onto the staircase, looking more intent than ever. Maybe she'd missed a knock at the door or the ring of a phone.

131

"Do you think there's been some breakthrough in the investigation?" she asked.

The curt jerk of his head could have meant anything, and his words had the same effect. "Let me go find out. I'll be back as soon as I can."

Her heart sank, but she forced a smile. "Okay."

He kissed her again, long enough for her to reciprocate. A deep, yearning kiss that pushed hope back into her. Whatever was wrong, it was with the outside world, not between him and her.

"Okay," she whispered when he broke away.

Chase nodded once and stepped out of view. Sophie sat curled up in the sheets, listening to the commotion as the dogs stirred. The door creaked open, then slammed, and silence returned.

She sat for another full minute, wrapped in the sheet, ready to cry. Then she forced herself to move. Crying didn't accomplish anything, and for all she knew, Chase might return quickly with good news.

So she descended, let the dogs out, and fed them, all while picturing herself and Chase having the morning she'd wished for. She looked around wistfully. Well, she'd start with breakfast, so when Chase returned, she'd have everything ready to go. Then she'd get dressed and do her hair — a waterfall braid — and then. . .

She did all that, then waited, and waited a little more. Finally, the door opened, and she jumped to her feet.

"Hi," she whispered.

"Hi," Chase said, standing still.

Sophie could have cried, because all the awkwardness they'd shed was back again.

"Anything new?" she asked at last.

He ran a hand through his hair, looking more tired than she'd ever seen him before. He opened his mouth then closed it again, fishing for words. "Yeah. Lots. First, we've heard from Officer Meli. The police have a suspect in custody. David."

She sank to the kitchen stool. Part of her had suspected all along, but she still couldn't believe it. "David?" Was he really capable of trying to kill her?

Chase nodded wearily. "I need to go to the police station to see exactly what they have on him. But, yeah. It's David, all right."

"I'll go."

Chase shook his head immediately. "I don't think that's a good idea. Do you?"

Sophie looked at her feet. What would she say to David? What would she do?

"I guess not," she admitted. When she looked up, Chase seemed more worried than ever before. "What is it?"

He forced a shrug, which didn't reassure her at all. "Another issue has come up. Nothing to do with you," he added quickly. "A security issue with the neighboring estate."

She studied him closely, but his guarded expression didn't give anything away. How serious an issue? What kind?

"Anyway, I need to check on that too." Chase looked over her shoulder, utterly glum. "Damn. You made breakfast and everything. I wish I didn't have to go."

She wanted to slam the door shut and lock away the outside world. But that wasn't the way life worked. Chase had a job to do, and he'd already devoted too much time to her.

"I wish too." She slid her hands over his arm. "But we can talk later. Right?"

He bit his lip, and she wondered why he looked so torn. "Yeah. Later. Will you wait for me?"

She rubbed her arms, thinking it over. She wasn't actually scheduled to work that day, and since the dogs were there with her...

"Sure," she said, trying to sound chipper but failing miserably.

They stood, looking at each other wordlessly, and Sophie felt a thousand regrets chug between them like a long train line. One after another, all chained to each other, stretching on and on. Chase shoved his hands deep into his pockets, not appearing the least bit ready to go. But a car horn beeped outside, and he looked up.

"Okay," he whispered, giving her a peck on the cheek. "See you."

"See you," she echoed, watching him go. Then she closed the door and stood there for a full five minutes, hoping to hear his footsteps rushing back to her.

The dogs looked at her mournfully, and all she heard was the wild rustling of the trees. A powerful wind had sprung up overnight, and the sky was a solid, mournful gray.

"I guess the forecast was right," she muttered.

Half an hour ticked by, but it felt like hours, and eventually, she motioned the dogs to the door. She would go crazy waiting around.

"How about we go for a short ride, guys?"

As always, the dogs were game, and off they went, up the path to the driveway where her beat-up Nissan stood. Dell had driven it over the previous evening, helping her once again. The keys were in the ignition, so she shooed the dogs into the back and drove off as quietly as she could. David was in custody, so there was no danger, and since there was an issue at the neighboring estate, she didn't want to disturb anyone. Besides, she needed some time alone in her special thinking place. It wasn't far, and on such a blustery day, there wouldn't be too many people around.

She drove north and eased her car over the bump where the pavement of the Honoapi'ilani Highway gave way to unfinished road. Then she followed the narrow, winding lane and parked at the turnout to the blowhole. As she hoped, there were no visitors. It was just her, the ocean, and the whipping wind. She zipped up her windbreaker and headed toward the blowhole, where she found a flat rock and settled down. The dogs wandered around, sniffing bushes and puddles, leaving her to her thoughts.

The problem was, her mind skipped all over the place, from heated memories of her night with Chase to the chilling news that David had been arrested. She wished she had asked Chase for more details. Was David accused of setting off the explosion *and* shooting at her?

The offshore wind whipped at her hair. She pulled on her hood and hunkered down. That raw, exposed coast suited her mood perfectly, and she was in no rush to go. Although David had been arrested, she felt no relief, only a deepened sense of mystery — and sadness. She'd come to Maui seeking goodness and joy, but David had cast a cloud so thick, she wondered if she would ever get out from under it.

Her locket warmed, and she brought it up to her eyes. At least there was that. Her aunt had insisted the little locket was a repository of goodness and love. And boy, did she need it.

Waves crashed against the rocky shoreline, and the blowhole erupted, sending a plume of water into the air. Boris skittered over and hid behind her legs, shaking.

"Don't worry." She rubbed his ears. "It does that all the time. Look."

A second, smaller burst followed the first, accompanied by a gurgling *whoosh!*

"Nothing to worry about."

Poor Boris remained huddled, unconvinced. When the blowhole went off again a few minutes later, covering them with a fine mist, he shuddered the same way.

"Stupid dog," someone laughed.

Sophie nearly jumped out of her skin. When she whirled to see who it was, she gasped.

"David?"

The noise of the wind and the waves had let him sneak up unnoticed. Darcy and Coco bustled to her side, growling.

She jumped to her feet, clutching her car keys, wishing she had something more substantial to defend herself with. "What are you doing here?"

"Aw, you know. Checking out the sights." David's eyes were fixed on her, not the blowhole, and a chill went down her spine.

Behind him, three men in suits picked their way down the rocks, looking out of place. The wind pulled at their ties and the flaps of their jackets as they moved. David grinned and repositioned the long black bag slung over his shoulder.

Darcy snarled, backing up until his rear bumped Sophie's legs, forming her last line of defense.

One desperate glance up to the road dashed her hopes — there was no one there to help. Just the dark SUV that David and the men must have arrived in, and no one else. Sophie stared. Who were they? What did they want? And whoa, wasn't David supposed to be in police custody?

When he stepped closer, she backed up, and he grinned.

"Aw, come on, Sophie. You don't have to be scared of me."

One look at his predatory eyes told her the opposite, and she kept backing away, splashing through the puddles left by the blowhole. Had the police released David? Had he escaped?

"What are you doing here?"

She glanced around, wondering how she might escape. The rock ledge only went so far before falling away into the crashing surf. Steel-gray clouds clogged the sky, and the wind dampened her cheeks with spray from a crashing wave.

"Well, I've got this problem, see?" David said. "And I'm looking to solve it."

Sophie sidestepped, turning in a slight circle rather than backing up to the very edge of the cliff. "And this problem is. . . ?"

David's face cracked into a smile. "You."

Somehow, he found that amusing, and she couldn't understand why. But then again, David had always been like that. Pulling the legs off beetles in order to watch them squirm. Kicking dogs for laughs. Shooting at rabbits and missing purposely, just to see them panic and flee.

"I'm the problem?" She tried keeping her voice even. Meanwhile, she calculated the distance to her car, but it seemed miles away.

"You're the problem and the solution at the same time." David laughed like that was the cleverest thing ever.

"I don't understand." She slipped a hand into her pocket and hit a couple of buttons on her phone, hoping they were the right ones. If she could somehow get hold of Chase or the police... Heck, she'd be happy to make contact with Mr. Lee at that point.

"Now, that's your problem," David said. "You just don't seem to understand."

"Then why don't you explain?" she said, though she wasn't sure she wanted to know.

He rolled his eyes. "I told you already. I need money. You have money. Simple."

"It's not my money."

"It is now that the old bat died."

She gaped. "Don't you call my aunt that!"

He sighed. "See? That's your problem. You're always getting attached. To that old lady. To your dumb dogs. To that guy you've been hanging around with." His face darkened. "All that makes you lose sight of the big picture."

She rubbed her arms. That line came right from her stepfather's playbook. And for him, the big picture was never anything good.

She circled the other way. "The big picture?"

Whoosh! The blowhole went off again, and the water drenched one of the three men, who glared as if it had been Sophie's fault.

"The big picture," David affirmed. "Your father's plan. Don't you want to make him proud?"

"Stepfather," she said. "And, no. I want nothing to do with his crazy ideas."

"His ideas weren't crazy. We need to defend ourselves. It's like Darwin said. Eat or be eaten. Live free or die."

Sophie made a face. " 'Live free or die' was John Stark."

"Whatever." David shrugged. "The point is, a vision takes money. That's where you come in."

Darcy growled a little louder, and Sophie grabbed some of that courage for herself. "No, that's where you go out and earn what you need."

A car appeared then disappeared around a curve in the road, making Sophie's hopes soar, only to fade.

David's face twisted. "Damn it, Sophie. You could make things a lot easier on yourself, you know."

She stuck her hands on her hips. "You mean, make things easier for you?"

"All you have to do is give me the money."

Sophie's jaw hung open. She'd had her suspicions, but now she was sure.

"You did it. You set off the explosion." She covered her mouth with her hand, still unable to fully accept that ugly truth. "You shot at me."

And David, the bastard, grinned like a Cheshire cat.

Sophie found her hands shaking with a mix of fear and anger. "I don't get it. Why didn't you just ask? Why bother making the truck blow up? Why bother shooting?"

A sly grin passed over David's face. "Those were just messages. You know, to make myself clear. If I wanted you dead, honey, you'd be dead."

Sophie gulped away a sob. She couldn't show fear. Not around David.

"And now that I have made myself clear. . . " he continued.

"Clear?" she practically screamed. "Nothing you say makes sense."

"You want me to spell it out for you? Fine. I want the money. I wanted you too, but now, I don't really care."

She snorted. Was she supposed to feel bad about that?

"And if I don't give you the money?"

He shrugged. "Then we go to Plan B. You know who's next in line to inherit your aunt's money?"

Sophie couldn't believe her ears. Was David serious?

"Your mother, that's who. And she knows to do the smart thing, unlike you."

Sophie wanted to scream. Her mother did the safe thing. She didn't ask questions, and she didn't think for herself. She just did as she was told.

"Listen to yourself," she said, trying to appeal to the boy she once knew.

"No, you listen to me. I need that money, and you are going to give it to me."

For a moment, she considered doing so. No amount of money was worth risking her life for. Still, what if David used it to harm others?

"What do you want it for?" She stuck her hands on her hips, more to bolster her own nerves than to impress David.

"With some things, sweetheart, it's better not to know."

Sophie stamped her foot. She might not be a warrior, but she wasn't a pushover. At least, not any more.

"Well, I want to know. I'm in charge of that money, after all."

She had a hard time not trembling after that, because it felt strange to issue an order instead of receiving one.

David's face twisted with annoyance, but he finally replied. "All right, then. Why the hell not?"

The three men behind him looked at each other, concerned. In the distance, something moved, and Sophie's heart leaped. A vehicle appeared, slowing to pull over on the side of the road. Chase's pickup!

She yanked her eyes away before David noticed. The more he talked, the more time Chase had to climb down and help her out of this mess.

"First, we need more space to train," David said. "To prepare. To launch our next operations from."

Sophie did her best to pay attention as Chase — and Dell, bless him — quietly picked their way down the rocky path from the roadside.

"A private place where we can make those upgrades your stepfather dreamed about." David made air quotes around *upgrades.*

Her surprise must have shown, because David grinned. "That's right, honey. The ultimate fighting machine. We're finally going to make that dream come true."

Her jaw dropped as David patted his bear claw necklace. Did he mean shape-shifting?

"Don't you remember what happened to Mike?" she breathed, keeping her voice low.

David shrugged. "I found a better way."

Sophie glanced at the other men. Wasn't David worried about them overhearing?

He laughed outright. "Ha. That's no secret with these guys. Meet Lamont, McGraw, and Vucovich — or should I say, my wolf buddy and his two friends, the bears."

Sophie froze. Was he serious?

The man on the right — McGraw — shot David a sharp look. "Watch what you say, asshole. The boss will have your hide if we don't pull this off quietly, like she ordered."

Sophie stared. McGraw's bulky, rounded shoulders and thick layer of stubble reminded her vaguely of Chase's brother, Tim. Vucovich was the same — built like a tank. With a little imagination, she could picture any of them turning into bears.

Please, no, she wanted to beg.

The other man — Lamont — was leaner and more agile, with medium-length brown hair that fell over his eyes. The way he shot sidelong glances this way and that made her think of images she'd seen of wolves in the wild in the early stages of a hunt. He had a wary, vigilant air to him. A little like Chase, in fact.

She took a step back, staring at the men. A werewolf? Two werebears?

Her mind filled with images of Mike's agonizing death, and she winced.

"It won't work. Remember Mike? The change killed him. It just isn't possible. Drop the idea, David. Please." Her voice was a whisper, and her hands shook.

David's smile turned even more sinister. "Aw, I knew you cared about me. But don't you worry. I've got someone who's going to help me do it right." He flexed his chest muscles as if already trying out a powerful new body.

Sophie glanced back at Chase, who was halfway down the path. Dell had broken away from him to come down from the right. Soon, they'd both be at her side and—

Her thoughts screeched to an abrupt stop. If David's accomplices really were shifters, Chase and Dell were in terrible danger. Not even a couple of elite Special Forces soldiers could fend off wild animals with their bare hands.

"So, I bet you're rethinking things right now," David went on, arrogant as ever. "You want to be on the winning side, right?" He grinned, all friendly again. "Just think it over, Sophie. We could start a new group. An offshoot of the Seventy-Sixers. We could be the ones everyone else looks up to."

She clenched her fists. David was crazy if he thought that changed her mind.

"The winning side?"

"Yep. My side, baby. The shifter side."

"And who exactly is the enemy?"

His face darkened. "The government. Big corporations. Any asshole who thinks they have the right to tell me what to do."

Whoosh! The blowhole exploded, accentuating David's point.

Darcy growled. Coco and Boris huddled against her legs. Chase and Dell had slowed to sneak up unnoticed, but any minute now...

"Show her, McGraw." David snapped his fingers.

McGraw threw him the evil eye. "I'm here on the boss's orders, not yours."

Sophie racked her mind for who that boss might be. They'd mentioned a woman. But who?

Lamont grinned and started loosening his tie. "What's the big deal?"

"Yeah," Vucovich added. "Think of it as a warm-up for the main job we came here for."

Sophie couldn't follow a word. What exactly did they have planned? And if she was just the warm-up, what was the main event?

She backed up as the dogs growled at the men.

"Try stopping me, you pups," Lamont sneered, taking his jacket off.

Seconds later, he unbuttoned his shirt and started loosening his belt. When Vucovich followed suit, Sophie blanched. God, was rape part of his plan?

"Don't get sidetracked," McGraw cautioned.

But David just egged the two men on. "Come on. Show her. It'll be fun."

Fun? It was more like a cruel trick.

The wind kept whipping strands of hair into Sophie's face, and she pulled them back to look around. Chase was crouched by a boulder behind Lamont, looking darker and more dangerous than she'd ever seen him. Dell wasn't far from McGraw, but did either realize what danger they were in?

Chase! she wanted to cry. *Help. Save me. No, wait — run away.*

Lamont untied his shoes and pushed his pants down. "Watch this, sweetheart. The real thing."

She didn't want to watch, but she couldn't tear her gaze away, because Lamont dropped to all fours and ducked his head. Darcy pranced forward two steps, barking madly, then skittered back to Sophie's legs.

"Yeah, watch, little guy," David laughed.

She prayed that it would all turn out to be a bad joke, but Lamont and Vucovich started making noises much like Mike had once done. Fur broke out all over their skin and grew thicker. When Mike had tried to shift, the fur had come and gone in uneven clumps, and his screams of pain never ceased. But Lamont and Vucovich shifted smoothly with nary a sound. Their ears tapered into triangles, and their noses darkened. She barely noticed the stages of their faces stretching, nor the way their limbs reshaped. One minute, Lamont was a man, and the next, he was a wolf. Vucovich was a bear. It was startling, but not horrifying. In fact, there was something magical about it all.

But then the wolf's eyes focused on her, showing pure blood lust.

"No," she whispered, inching to one side.

Yes, the wolf seemed to say, showing off its long, pointy fangs.

David chuckled like a madman. "Soon, I'll be able to do that too. And then—"

He whirled as Chase stepped out from behind the rocks. Sophie nearly cried out in relief, but she choked with fear.

What could Chase possibly do?

Chase edged around the rock, working his way toward Sophie.

"Stop," he growled, addressing the wolf. "Stop right now."

Chapter Fifteen

Sophie froze as Chase held out his hands, showing he didn't want a fight. But his eyes glowed in a way she'd never seen before, turning the hazel into a fiery brick color. They were full of anger, but full of regret too. Why?

"This is our territory, and you know it," Chase barked at Vucovich and McGraw. Then he faced David. "You have no idea who you're getting mixed up with." He jerked a thumb toward the road. "Last chance to get out."

David laughed. "Or what?"

"Or die." Chase's voice was bitter and worn. The voice of a man who'd seen enough death and destruction for one lifetime.

"Oh yeah? You're going to get rid of us all by yourself?"

"No," Chase said simply as Dell stepped into view near McGraw. Gone was the happy-go-lucky jokester; this Dell was a furious warrior, ready to do battle.

Chase pointed. "Him, me, plus my brothers. They'll be here soon."

Sophie's hopes swelled at the thought of everyone rushing over to help. But there was no sign of movement on the road above, and she feared that would be too late.

Lamont's paws splashed through puddles as he took a step forward, cutting Sophie off from Chase.

"Stop," she shouted, hoping the wolf would understand. "This is crazy."

"It's not crazy. It's destiny," David crowed.

Chase shook his head. "Destiny? This is not destiny."

His gaze traveled to Sophie, and his glowing eyes softened.

Love, she thought, warming. *That's the color of love.*

Then she glanced at Lamont, and behind him, Vucovich. Their eyes were glowing too, although in a murderous hue. Sophie tilted her head as scattered thoughts slowly came together in her mind like pieces of a puzzle. Not enough to click into place, just to hint at an outline.

What? She wanted to scream. *What's the connection?*

"I've had it with this asshole." David snapped his fingers. "Kill him. I'll take care of her."

Sophie's hands shook. David meant it. So did Lamont, whose canine eyes signaled something like *I'll kill with pleasure.*

"Chase," she warned, willing him to run away.

He turned to her with a look so conflicted, so full of mourning, she nearly cried.

"I love you, Sophie."

Her heart ached. Why did that sound so much like goodbye?

"I love you too," she whispered.

Chase went on as if he hadn't heard. "Please don't hate me for this."

How could she hate him for rushing to her assistance? "I could never—"

Then all the color drained out of her face, because Chase's face twisted, and the shirt split down his back. "Don't hate me," he repeated in a lower, strained tone.

Sophie covered her mouth, stifling a cry. Hair broke out all over Chase's skin as he shook off the scraps of his clothes. His fingers curled and meshed, and his frown stretched, revealing ever pointier teeth. His ears pulled back, and his limbs bent...

"No," Sophie whispered. It couldn't be.

David cackled as Darcy barked furiously. "I guess lover boy never mentioned he was a shifter, huh?"

Sophie stared in disbelief. The gentle, caring man she'd spent the night with had just turned into a wolf. One that balanced on his back legs before dropping to all fours as if to hammer in a point. Human. Beast. Shifter.

"Chase?" she whispered.

A beast with chestnut fur, exactly the color of Chase's hair. His canine eyes were filled with love, at least for the moment that they fixed on her. But then he swung his head toward Lamont, and the glow turned deadly again.

Coco whimpered, and Sophie nearly did too. Darcy stood perfectly still, staring between Chase and the other wolf, almost as if choosing sides. Sophie gripped his collar tightly. The little dog was all heart, but he didn't belong in the middle of a wolf fight.

Then Sophie shrieked as Lamont rushed at Chase, who leaped to ward him off. God, no.

"Finally, a little action," David cackled.

A *little* action? All Sophie saw was a blur as the wolves jumped at each other, splashing through shallow puddles left by the blowhole. Their claws extended, and their lips drew back to expose long white canines. Their bodies collided in midair. When they crashed to the rocks, they rolled, sprang apart, and leaped at each other's throats again.

Sophie had witnessed several dog fights, but she couldn't believe the wolves' ferocity and power. They were much bigger, and much deadlier, than dogs. More experienced, too. Every move the wolves made was aimed at murder, not for show.

Vucovich, the bear, watched them closely, ready to leap into the fight when an opening presented itself.

McGraw cursed and loosened his tie.

"You don't need to get involved," Dell warned, cutting him off from the others. "Cut your losses and leave."

McGraw rolled his eyes. "Right. Sure."

Darcy barked wildly. Sophie grabbed him by the collar, as much to anchor herself in reality as to hold the dog back from the fight.

The darker-colored wolf — Chase — sidestepped Lamont's attack and slashed at his shoulder, drawing blood. Then Chase dropped back and paused, giving his enemy one more chance to reconsider. But Lamont shook himself, snarled, and rushed forward again, intent on a fight to the death.

"Damn it," David muttered to McGraw. "I thought Moira said you guys were the best."

Sophie furrowed her brow. She couldn't recall a Moira from back home. Had a new woman joined the militia?

"Moira," Dell spat. "Should have known."

"Get in there. Help him," David ordered McGraw.

The burly man had his arms crossed firmly over his chest, but eventually, he relented. "I will — but just to get things moving. Don't lose sight of what we're really here for."

"What *you're* really here for," David muttered under his breath.

But McGraw didn't seem to hear. He removed his jacket and tie and laid them methodically aside in unrushed movements, totally unlike the wolf fight raging beside him.

Darcy aimed his barks at McGraw. Sophie watched with sick fascination as McGraw shifted into bear form without so much as a grunt. Fur sprouted uniformly, and he remained balanced easily on two feet.

Shifting doesn't have to be gruesome, David had said, and maybe he was right. McGraw's transition was totally fluid, almost graceful. The kind of process Sophie had envisioned when she had naïvely imagined becoming a shifter as a child.

But she had imagined furry creatures frolicking in the woods, not raging beasts with claws and inch-long fangs. The bear stood for one moment, letting the wind ruffle his fur. Then he lumbered toward the sparring wolves and—

"Last chance," Dell muttered, blocking his way.

Sophie wanted to scream. Was Dell insane?

Then her eyes bulged, because Dell started shifting too. She stared as tawny features emerged from the blend of human and animal shapes.

"What?" she gasped.

She'd always thought of Dell as a Viking, what with his long, golden hair and thick beard. But never, ever as a lion.

"Dell?" she whispered in shock.

The lion shook out his mane and roared, making Coco and Boris cower. McGraw growled back, but the grizzly didn't advance. He just stood there, hemmed in by Dell, watching the fight unfold.

Which still left Chase facing a wolf and a bear on his own, not to mention David, who unslung his shoulder bag and took out a rifle. He screwed the stock and barrel together, muttering all the time.

"You want something done, you have to do it yourself."

Sophie's heart clenched. God, no.

She checked the road, hoping to see Chase's friends springing out of a car, all armed to the teeth. But there was no one there. The thought did make another piece of the puzzle click into place in her mind, though. Dell was a shifter, and so was Chase. Did that mean his brothers were as well? And what about Anjali, Hailey, and the others?

For a moment, she felt cheated, even lied to. But that all faded away when she pictured each of them. Connor was friendly and polite, and Tim was always kind. Dell was funny and upbeat. All of them doted on their girlfriends with a kind of adoring devotion few men showed, and they had all jumped to help her after the explosion at the smoothie truck.

Her heart swelled. All those strangers had been so kind to her. It was David, the boy she'd grown up with, she couldn't trust.

The locket warmed on her chest, and a voice drifted through her mind.

You can trust them. You can trust love.

Sophie looked at Chase. It was easy to love the man. But to love a wolf?

Something jerked her hand, and she yanked her attention back to her feet. Darcy had just broken out of her grasp.

"Darcy, wait!" she cried, but it was too late. Darcy splashed through a puddle, headed directly for the bear advancing on Chase.

Coco and Boris filled the air with frantic barks that said, *You're just a little guy. That bear is huge,* but Darcy didn't seem to care.

The bear — Vucovich — changed direction, coming directly for Darcy. Sophie lunged for a rock then threw it with all her might. She expected the rock to bounce harmlessly off the bear's shoulder, but it landed with a thump, and the beast stumbled back. Then it glared at her with its lips peeled back as if to say, *You're next, sweetheart.*

Her pulse raced. What she nuts to provoke a bear like that? Then again, that was Darcy out there, not to mention Chase and Dell. All of them were risking their lives for her.

Darcy jumped into position beside Chase, having made up his mind about which side to support. It was almost laughable, seeing the little terrier face off with a wolf and a bear, but Sophie's heart warmed. That little dog had all the courage in the world, and he was the most loyal soul she knew.

Just like Chase, that little voice said.

Heat radiated through her chest as she stared at Chase's dark brown pelt. He had done so much and asked for so little. Finally, she understood what he'd been meaning to say but couldn't quite get out.

But, holy cow. The man she loved was a wolf?

Vucovich rumbled and stepped forward, setting off the next onslaught. Lamont jumped ahead of him, and Chase braced himself for the onslaught. When the two wolves crashed together, the bear followed. Darcy did too, yapping and nipping to distract the bear. The grizzly swiped at Darcy, who barely jumped clear in time.

Sophie hurled another rock at the bear. That one bashed into the bear's brow, producing another furious roar. Then she reached down for another and—

"Would you quit that?" David snapped, grabbing her arm.

She twisted, trying to break free, but her feet slipped out from under her.

David cursed, kicking Coco and Boris away. They weren't the warriors that Darcy was, but they did snap at David's ankles, protecting her as best they could.

Sophie found herself engulfed in chaos. Dogs barking, beasts growling, water splashing. The blowhole erupted with a thunderous blast, soaking them all. Sophie blinked, trying to clear the jumble in her mind.

Keep your head clear. Her stepfather's drill sergeant voice sounded in her mind, loud and clear. He'd always said that during the exercises he'd put everyone through like involuntary recruits in his private army. *Panic is the enemy.*

Never in her wildest dreams had Sophie imagined she'd find those lessons useful, and certainly not in a situation like this. But there she was, lying at the feet of a madman while wild animals tore at each other only a few feet away. She took a deep breath and dug a little deeper through those unwanted memories. David was bigger and stronger. Worse, he had a weapon. But she had been trained for that, right? She pushed one foot forward and the other back, bracing herself. With a quick twist and a dip of one shoulder, she yanked David's arm down and—

"Hey!" he blurted as she judo-rolled him over her shoulder and let him crash to the ground.

Sophie stared, amazed it had actually worked.

The rifle had clattered to one side, and she leaped forward to kick it out of David's reach. When David rushed after it, a shadowy memory rushed through Sophie's mind. She'd slipped, but before she knew it, she was rolling into a scissor kick that knocked David right off his feet. Then she raced toward the road with Coco and Boris at her heels. She wasn't sure whether to feel proud or sick that all the paramilitary training she'd been forced to undertake was still mired in her soul, even after all that time.

"You bitch!" David yelled, lunging for her.

The dogs tripped him up, allowing Sophie to get a step ahead. If she could somehow get there and jump into her car—

With a gasp, she pulled up short. Vucovich had cut away from the wolf fight and planted himself firmly in her path, daring her to come closer.

"Leave her to me," David ordered, hurrying up behind her.

A howl sounded from the left, and Sophie looked around. One of the wolves stood over the other, sinking its teeth into the other's neck. They were both matted with blood, and her heart leaped. Which was Chase?

It took ten agonizing seconds to figure out which wolf was which. The beast struggling on the ground was Lamont, and the victor was Chase.

Lamont ceased struggling and went still. Chase held on for another few seconds before releasing his hold on the enemy.

Lamont dropped like a stone, unmoving. Dead?

Dead, Darcy's haughty sniff seemed to say.

Sophie felt sick.

Chase swung his head toward her with an expression so full of regret, it broke her heart.

Forgive me, his eyes begged. *Don't hate me for who I am. For what I must do to save you.*

Sophie stared. For the briefest of moments, her focus sharpened like never before.

"Chase," she whispered.

Fear and surprise swirled around the edges of her heart, but love filled most of that space.

Love is the most powerful force on earth, her aunt had once said. *And when you know, you really know.*

Sophie sucked in a deep breath, reasoning it out. She loved Chase. Did it really matter if he was man or wolf?

Up to that point, McGraw had hung back from the fight, hemmed in by Dell, the lion. Then the bear rumbled and attacked Dell. Meanwhile, the second bear reared to his hind feet, looming over Chase.

"That will be me someday," David growled as he caught up to Sophie and grabbed her from behind. "Only better."

The bear claw necklace dug into her back, and he held her wrists tightly with one hand. The other slapped over her chest, covering her locket.

"Oh yes. I'll be needing this too," David muttered.

Sophie stiffened. Why would he be interested in her locket? Then her mind went into hyperdrive. There was no way she would let David have the locket. It seemed imperative somehow.

On instinct, Sophie stamped on his foot and lurched away.

"Damn it," David cursed, coming after her.

With a wolf and a bear blocking one way out and a lion/bear fight cutting off the other, Sophie had no choice but to rush to the edge of the cliff. The blowhole erupted, drenching her. Water plastered her hair to her face, and she stumbled to her knees an inch from the rock's edge. She peered over the sheer drop. No way could she jump to escape.

"Where you going to go now?" David sneered, smacking her head from behind.

The blow sent her reeling to one side. Her shoulder smashed into rock, and she cried out. A wolf howled, and she knew it was Chase. But when she looked up, all she could see was the hulking form of the grizzly, looming before him.

"No," she mumbled, scrambling to her feet.

But she'd hit her head in the fall, and everything unfolded in a slow blur. Coco and Boris whimpered and barked, forming a cloud of brown and white near her feet. David was there too, reaching for the rifle with what looked like two right hands.

Hurry, a voice whispered as the locket flared with heat. *Knock it away.*

She focused just in time to see Vucovich slash at Chase's shoulder with huge, raking claws. The bear moved in for the kill as Chase rolled to the ground. But Darcy — brave, indomitable Darcy — rushed in, sinking his teeth into the grizzly's rear leg. The bear roared and twisted, swatting Darcy away.

"Darcy!" Sophie screamed as the dog flew across the rocks and landed with a crash. He landed in a heap, unmoving.

"Fucking dog," David muttered as he closed in on the rifle.

Coco and Boris rushed over to Darcy. Anger welled up in Sophie — or was that hate? Emotions she'd banished for so long, pushing aside all the love she'd painstakingly gathered over the past months.

Without thinking, she kicked the rifle out of David's hands. It clattered over the rocks then went flying over the cliff.

"You bitch!" David screamed, too late.

Sophie jumped to her feet and held up her fists. For the first time in her life, she understood why hate was so powerful, and why men like David got such a high from tapping in to it. But something warmed on her chest. The moment she touched the locket, love rushed back into her heart, extinguishing the hate. The locket was so hot, she nearly jerked her hand away, but that heat didn't burn. It just flowed into her, filling her with a different source of power.

Love. The most powerful thing there is, her aunt had once said.

And, wow. Sophie believed it. She clasped the locket tightly.

"How dare you?" David yelled.

"How dare you?" she screamed back, trying to assess the situation. Chase and Vucovich battled on in a tight knot. Dell and McGraw covered huge swaths of territory, leaping at each other, then retreating. They were a good twenty yards away, with the distance increasing steadily. That left David, who—

Sophie gasped as he wrenched her hand to her side. "Now I've had it. Choose. Life or death, Sophie. Which will it be?"

"Chase," she declared, still struggling. "I choose Chase."

David snorted. "That ain't an option, honey. It's me or nothing."

Heat radiated through her chest, and a gurgling sound came from behind David, signaling that the blowhole was about to interrupt. Sophie's gaze fell to the gaping hole only a few feet away.

David laughed. "I guess you choose death. Too bad."

He leaned in, focusing on her neck. His eyes brightened as if already relishing how good it would feel to squeeze the life out of her. To ignore her choked pleas and watch her slowly die. He would give her a little shake and — ugh — kiss her cheek as the life seeped out of her body. Then, with one cold gesture, he would shove her body off the cliff.

All that played out in David's eyes. But at the same time, another vision unfolded in Sophie's mind. A vision of Chase, looking down at her as they lay together in bed. His soft kiss, his gentle caress. All that love and all that yearning aimed at her.

She gritted her teeth. David was right. It was life or death, and she had to choose.

Her eyes slid from David to the gurgling blowhole.

Warning. Stay clear of blowhole. You can be sucked in and killed.

David leaned in to choke her, and Sophie rocked back, using the slippery surface to catch him off-balance. Then, summoning all the energy she had, she shoved the other way. *Really* shoved, with more force than she had ever summoned in her life.

David sprawled backward, grunting in surprise. He teetered at the edge of the blowhole for a moment, and Sophie held her breath as he glanced down. When his eyes slid back to Sophie, there was murder written in them.

"That's it," David grunted. "You're going to wish—"

His words were drowned out by the slosh of water, and Coco — little, helpless Coco — jumped at his shins, pushing him back. It wasn't much, and David easily stuck out his right foot to catch himself on the other side of the hole. But the gurgle became a roar, and David's look turned from one of annoyance to panic.

Whoosh, the blowhole went.

David flailed, surrounded by water that shot up with the force of a firehose. Then the water dropped, and David dropped too. One minute, he was there, and the next, the water had dragged him out of sight.

"David," Sophie half whispered, half yelped.

Coco had been thrown aside by the eruption, but when it ceased, she shook her fur and peered down into the hole.

"Coco!" Sophie gestured wildly, and the mutt scampered back to her side.

Sophie stared at the blowhole then scanned the sea. Would David be dragged out there? Could he possibly survive?

Then a roar sounded behind her, and she whirled to face the shifter fight.

Chapter Sixteen

Sophie turned just in time to see Chase being thrown against the rocks. His wolf body was battered, and Vucovich bled from several deep wounds too. But the grizzly had the upper hand, and it was closing in for the kill.

"No!"

She grabbed a rock and rushed forward, hurling it at the bear. The mighty beast turned and growled at her, ignoring Chase. So she threw another rock and another. Each successive blow drew a greater reaction from the grizzly, who winced, ducked, and roared.

One little part of her mind registered that she shouldn't be able to make such an impact. That something other than pure panic might be fueling her. But then the grizzly came straight for her, and she froze, staring death in the face.

Then Darcy — dear little Darcy, limping up like a canine Napoleon who didn't know when to quit — sank his teeth into the bear's back leg. The beast twisted around to chase him away, leaving its neck unguarded. Chase struggled to his feet and lunged in with his jaws wide open.

The grizzly's ruff had to be incredibly thick, but once the wolf sank his teeth in, he refused to let go. Neither did Darcy, who hung on as the bear flailed around. At first, the beast seemed merely annoyed. But the wolf's fangs must have sunk deeper, because the bear's movements became more desperate. With a mighty shake, it launched Darcy into the air. The Jack Russell crashed against a rock and fell, limp.

"Darcy!" Sophie screamed.

She nearly rushed over to him, but there was no time. Without Darcy's distraction, the grizzly could concentrate on

157

mauling Chase with its claws.

So, move. Help Chase, she ordered herself.

She screamed and waved, ignoring the instinct to flee. If Darcy could face a beast that big, she could bring herself to do the same.

The bear whirled and swiped at her, making the air whoosh in front of her face. Chase still hung on to its neck, and blood matted both their chests. Sophie nearly fled, but she found the strength to rush forward again, screaming at the beast. The more the bear focused on her, the more time Chase had to drain the life out of it.

"Over here," she shouted, grabbing another rock.

The bear glanced up as she launched the rock with power and accuracy that shocked her. When it struck the bear's muzzle, the beast howled and arched back.

Coco barked, as if cheering Chase on. *Now! Get him!*

The wolf clamped its jaws even harder, and the bear released a final, fading roar. Then it dropped to its side in a strange, slow-motion way, kicked a few times, and finally went limp. For a while, the only sound was that of waves crashing into rocks. Then the wolf released the bear and lurched away. After three shaky steps, it collapsed.

Sophie stumbled backward, landed on her rear, and sat there, staring. Her heart pounded all the louder for the surrounding silence. But when she reached for her locket, she found herself back on her feet, rushing toward Chase. She kneeled over him and—

She froze, and her hands shook an inch away from touching him. That wasn't just a wild beast. It was a werewolf — the kind of beast that had horrified her for so long.

Not just a werewolf, a corner of her mind reminded her. *It's Chase.*

Coco came up beside her, sniffing warily.

She whirled, because Dell and the other bear were still out there. Then she exhaled, because the lion was chasing McGraw into full retreat. McGraw had never fully committed himself to the fight, and now he was cutting his losses, it seemed.

Sophie turned back to Chase, petrified. How bad were his injuries?

Slowly, she reached out and touched the wounded wolf's sides. The fur was softer than she had imagined, and it was easy to recall running her fingers through Chase's hair.

"Chase," she whispered, caressing his wolf ears.

It really was him, and he'd risked everything for her. But he was totally, terrifyingly still.

A tear rolled down her cheek, followed by another. More followed, and soon, a whole river of tears blinded her while she whispered his name.

"Chase. . ."

She didn't know how long she sobbed for the man she loved, and for Darcy. For everything, it seemed like. The greatest sorrows of her life all welled up at the same time, and she felt lost.

Then a callused finger brushed her cheek, and she blinked. "Chase?"

The wolf was gone, and the man lay in its place.

"Sophie," he croaked.

A drop of water hung from his brow, and his hair was wet, just like the wolf's had been.

She held her breath. Was Chase really back? Then she gasped at his wounds. His left shoulder was torn open, and four parallel claws raked across his chest. But Chase just cupped her cheek and stroked it with his thumb.

"Are you okay? Please tell me you're okay," she begged.

"I'm okay," he rasped. "And sorry. I'm so sorry."

She wiped away her tears and hugged him as carefully as she could. "Sorry for what?"

"For everything."

She straightened. "You saved me. Again. I'm the one who should be sorry. You were trying to tell me, weren't you?" Her stomach lurched. "Please don't tell me it was something else. Something bigger than this."

He shook his head. "Just the shifter part. No other surprises, I swear." Then he clasped her hand and looked up at her so warily, it broke her heart. "But what about—"

She shook her head. "I love you, Chase. Nothing else matters."

Sure, she'd need some time to swallow the whole wolf shifter thing. But nothing would shake her love for him.

"Nothing," she whispered, hugging him.

She could have stayed there forever, listening to his heart thump. But when she cracked open her eyes, she caught sight of the blood on his chest, and the reality of the situation slammed into her again. She sat back and fluttered her hands helplessly, staring at his wounds.

"Oh God. We have to stop the bleeding. . . "

Chase grasped her hands, calming her down. "It will be okay. We heal fast."

We meant *shifters*, she reckoned, but all that mattered to her was that he would be all right.

Roars sounded in the distance, and Sophie cringed. Part of that sound was the call of victory, but the other was the last gasp of death.

She gripped Chase's hand. "Was that Dell or the bear?"

"Dell," Chase said. "I mean, he got the bear. I mean. . . "

Sophie closed her eyes, trying not to picture the details. Then her eyes flew open in panic, and she whirled around.

"Darcy!"

The dog was lying where he'd been thrown by the grizzly, completely still. Boris stood near him, sniffing the air, afraid to approach.

Sophie rushed over. "Darcy. . . "

Slowly, carefully, she cradled him, and the tears returned when he didn't react.

"My sweet, brave Darcy. . . " she mumbled, rocking him helplessly. She could barely see through her tears, and the heat emanating from the locket increased.

How Chase had summoned the energy to limp over, she didn't know. She just wished Darcy had the healing powers of a shifter. His pulse was weak, his body motionless. Was she witnessing the final moments of Darcy's life?

"Talk to him," Chase whispered. "Tell him."

Her throat felt too thick to speak, but she choked out a few words. "My brave, brave Darcy. Such a good dog."

Hope drained out of her. It could only be a matter of time now. She closed her eyes and thought of "Rainbow Bridge" — the children's poem that described dog heaven in simple yet beautiful terms. Usually, the idea comforted her, but it did little to help now. Her eyes stung, and her heart ached.

"Darcy..." she sobbed, holding him close.

Something brushed Sophie's elbow, but she didn't care. Not even when it brushed her a second time. But the third time...

She glanced down. Wait. Was his tail wagging? She held her breath.

Darcy's eyes cracked open, and he licked her hand. So weakly, it scared her, but hope rushed into her at the same time.

"Good boy, Darcy," she cried, petting him gently. "Good boy."

Heat pulsed through her arm, and she closed her eyes, tracing it in her mind. That was her locket, not just giving her strength, but pouring into Darcy, too. Was that just love at work there, or something more?

Darcy's eyes slid shut again, which terrified her, but Chase touched her back. "Tough little guy. He's going to make it."

"How can you tell?"

Chase bit his lip. "Um... I can just tell. Just keep holding him."

Oh, she'd hold him, all right. Just like she'd hold Chase when she got the chance.

"Are you sure?" she squeaked.

Chase nodded. "I'm sure."

His eyes flashed, reminding her of the wolf, and suddenly, Sophie understood. Not the details, perhaps, but the gist of it. Dogs could communicate with one another, so wolves probably could too.

Coco and Boris came up to lick Darcy, and Sophie petted them, laughing and crying at the same time. She gripped Chase's hand, and the heat from the locket extended in that direction as well.

Love is the most powerful force on earth...

Sophie had certainly experienced her moments of doubt. But now, she was sure. Love really could conquer all.

Then footsteps scraped over the rocks, and her heart leaped. She looked up, frightened of who that might be. But when the familiar faces of Chase's friends came into view, she exhaled. Tim was the first to approach, followed by Hailey. Anjali wasn't far behind, though she cut over to intercept Dell, who was limping back, still in lion form.

"You okay, man?" Tim asked, looking more serious than she'd ever seen him.

Chase nodded slowly.

"What about Darcy?" Hailey asked, coming over to Sophie.

Sophie stroked his smooth, damp fur. "I think he's going to be okay."

Hailey came closer, looking between Sophie and Chase. Then she tilted her head and asked, ever so softly, "What about you?"

Sophie bit her lip. *Shaken up* didn't begin to describe how she felt, especially at the thought that Hailey and the others were probably shifters. Her heart hammered away as she studied their features closely.

A moment later, she shook the thought away. Shifter or not, it didn't matter. Their love for Chase was palpable, and they'd proven their kindness to her again and again.

"Sophie?" Hailey asked, concerned.

Sophie looked at Darcy then at Chase, who squeezed her hand. God, did she love him.

"I'm okay," she whispered, keeping her eyes firmly on Chase. "Really okay."

Chapter Seventeen

Chase woke slowly, still not quite ready to believe. A week had passed since that awful day on the rocks — the day he could have lost Sophie. He could be forgiven for holding her close all night long and not wanting to let her go now that it was morning, right?

"Mmm," she sighed, snuggling closer.

Coco and Boris snuggled up, and Chase sighed. But, hell. He could deal with a couple of dogs at the foot of the bed.

"Heya, buddy," he murmured, reaching down to pet Darcy, who didn't even flinch. In fact, he seemed to like it.

The little Jack Russell had spent the night on a pillow directly beside the couch — the plushest, biggest pillow to be found. It was huge, and the golden tassels at the corners made Darcy look like a goddamn maharajah. Anjali had brought it over sometime after the fight, and Sophie had spent the first forty-eight hours afterward fussing over both him and the dog.

Chase looked up at the loft. His injuries made climbing up out of the question at first, so they'd bunked out in the living room. He'd patched up pretty quickly, but they'd kept sleeping on the sofa bed to keep an eye on Darcy. Now that he was past the worst, Chase had hopes of moving up to the loft come nightfall. The dogs would have to stay at ground level, but they could live with that.

I'm alpha of our little pack, he explained to Darcy. *But you're my lieutenant, and you're in charge down here. The one who makes sure no bad guys get past you. Can I count on you?*

Darcy wagged his tail. *Yes, sir.*

Chase petted Darcy's ears, careful to avoid his wounds. The little guy had been slow to warm to him at first, but everything had changed since the fight, when they'd faced a common enemy to save Sophie.

Couldn't have done it without you, man, he said into the dog's mind.

Darcy flashed a smug little grin then closed his eyes. It would be a while until he could truly take on guard dog duties, but he would be all right.

And as for Sophie...

She saved herself, a little voice murmured in Chase's mind.

He ran a hand over his mate's side. So much had gone wrong, but somehow, it had ended up all right. On the morning before the fight, he'd hurried to the police station, only to discover they'd booked the wrong man. When he'd rushed home, Sophie was gone. His pack mates were getting ready to hunt down the shifter intruders, who had eluded Connor and Jenna on Oahu by leaving a false trail. That left Chase and Dell to catch up with Sophie, and they'd had no choice but to take on the intruders without waiting for backup.

The memories were ugly, but Sophie had been amazing, keeping her wits and fighting with incredible grit. She'd judo-flipped a full-grown man, for goodness' sake, and that pull-push move she'd managed to propel David toward the blowhole with had been pretty impressive too.

Where'd you learn that? he'd asked at one point in the past few days.

Sophie had made a face. *As a kid, I had to learn a lot of things I never wanted to use.*

She glanced down at her locket and moved her lips as if to add something, but in the end, she didn't speak.

His eyes dropped to where the locket rested against her bare skin. At times, he'd felt power surge from it. He'd concluded that was a byproduct of his muddled, love-struck mind. But now, he wasn't so sure.

Still, he wasn't ready to ask any more questions. Sophie had already revealed plenty, telling him all the details of the militia she'd grown up in. All the morning marches, all the training, all the crazy propaganda that she'd left behind.

My aunt was my shining light throughout that whole time. The only voice reminding me there was love in the world, not just fear and hate.

Chase had kissed her hand. *You sure learned the love part right.*

That brought her smile back, and they'd spent a good ten minutes hugging to reinforce it all.

Love, his wolf murmured.

Chase nodded along. Love really was the most powerful force of all.

He'd had the chance to open up to Sophie too, explaining about his childhood. Or rather, his puphood, seeing as he'd grown up in a wolf pack. He'd been scared that would turn Sophie off, but she'd been fascinated by every detail.

You mean, you got to howl at the moon and everything?

That had made him laugh and hug her again. Of course, it made sense that a woman who loved dogs could relate, but still. He couldn't believe his luck.

We don't howl at the moon. We howl to it. Someday, I'll show you.

She seemed to like the thought of that, and he brightened again. She'd mourned at the details, though. How grueling life in the wild could be, and how difficult it had been for him to transition to his new life. How often he'd thought of turning his back on the human world.

I know what you mean, she'd sighed. *Humans can really suck sometimes. But there are moments of such beauty too.*

Love. Beauty. Sunshine. They were all easier to find with Sophie around.

He looked at the ceiling. Never had he felt more firmly in the human world. The possibility of going feral had vanished for good.

In the end, he'd managed to tell Sophie everything he'd been holding back. He explained about shifters and mates, and how easily shifting came to them. He'd also told her about different shifter species: wolves like him, bears like Tim, lions like Dell, and dragons like Connor.

Sophie had gone pale at the mention of dragons, but she hadn't run screaming. She had just taken a deep breath, nodded, and quietly processed that information.

"Nice dragons?" she'd whispered after a long pause.

He held her closer. "Really nice. I promise."

She'd pressed herself to his chest even more tightly after that. But eventually, she went back to asking about wolves. Questions that didn't come from fear so much as curiosity and even. . . envy?

I'd love to run free like that, she'd sighed, making his hopes swell.

And now. . .

Chase looked down as Sophie stretched in his arms and looked at him through luminous, forest-green eyes.

"What are you thinking about?" she whispered.

He kissed her softly. "You. Me. How lucky I am."

They'd had time to talk about everything — and not just the big things. Sophie shared all kinds of little details, like her favorite colors and flowers. The stuffed animals she used to have, and her first day at work on that farm in Vermont. He'd told her about moving into the top bunk in the room he, Tim, and Connor had shared as teens, and he'd rambled on about some of the pranks his brothers had pulled in the military. It was amazing, how that felt like a lifetime ago. Everyone had grown up since then — becoming more serious, finding mates, settling down.

His grin stretched. That was him now too.

Sophie touched his cheek. "Did you sleep better last night?"

He nodded firmly. And how. The first few nights after the fight, he'd been in too much pain to sleep well. Then he'd been haunted by nightmares about poachers hunting his home pack. But out of nowhere came the best news he could possibly wish for. Tim was friends with a bear shifter clan in Arizona that ran a funky little place called the Blue Moon Saloon. A branch of that clan had moved to Montana, and they had rushed over to check on Chase's home pack. According to them, whatever poachers had been around were gone or keeping a low profile. Still, Todd Voss and his mixed band of shifters had vowed to stick around, making sure the danger really was gone.

"Tim said we can count on Todd and his clan. If anyone can sniff out trouble, they can."

Sophie drew a lazy circle on his chest. "The Blue Moon Saloon. I love the sound of it. We really have to visit someday."

Every time Sophie said *we*, Chase's smile grew. And when she talked about shifters in a positive light — especially bear shifters, who she'd had such a negative impression of for so long — his soul rejoiced.

He kissed her hand. "Maybe on the way to Montana."

"Someday." Sophie smiled. Then she sighed and fingered her locket absently. "Once we get things settled here, I guess."

His inner wolf wagged its tail. *Getting settled. That means mating.*

Chase held his tongue. There were a lot of aspects to *getting settled*, and he didn't want to rush Sophie. She had a long enough list as it was.

"I have to talk to Mr. Lee," Sophie said, looking off into the distance.

She was dead set on returning to work at Sunshine Smoothies, and now that the danger from David had passed, Chase couldn't really object. In truth, he loved the idea of her being close to the Lucky Devil. They could commute to work together, visit at break times...

He reined in his imagination before it took off.

Gotta mate first, his wolf insisted. *Make her ours forever.*

He wanted to — desperately — but he'd need time to break the details of mating to Sophie. He figured she wouldn't have a problem with the *forever* part, but wouldn't a nice girl like her balk at the idea of a mating bite delivered at the height of sex? And, crap. How exactly would he phrase all that?

So, we have to get naked, have sex, and just when we're both about to come, I bite you...

He blushed just thinking about saying such a thing aloud.

"And it's high time to go check with my aunt's lawyer," Sophie said, looking troubled.

That made him smile. He loved so many things about Sophie, and that was one. She knew the value of money, but she didn't make it the center of her world.

"Then I can research good causes to donate it to," she added, brightening.

He chuckled out loud. "What if it's a lot of money?"

She shrugged. "Then I can donate to several groups. I was thinking about the animal shelter, for starters..."

Most people would shake their heads at such a crazy suggestion, but Chase thought it was great. He listened to her mull over ideas for a while, then drifted off into a pleasant haze. But then Sophie said something else, and he stared. Whoa. Had she just brought up mating, or was his wolf messing with his mind?

"Um...say again?" he managed.

She blushed and looked down. They were both naked because they'd made love the previous night. Sweet, slow sex Chase could have spent the whole day dreaming about — or better yet, trying out a few more times.

Lots more times, his wolf insisted, going all dreamy again.

Chase blinked the thought away, trying to focus on what Sophie was mumbling. He cocked his head, still not catching her words.

Finally, she sighed and play-smacked him on his shoulder. "I said mating. That's also on my to-do list."

His eyes went wide, and his cheeks grew hot.

His inner wolf jumped to attention. *She said mating. So get to it already.*

"You...want that?" he asked, terrified he'd somehow misunderstood.

She looped her arms around his neck. "Of course, I want that. I want to be yours, and I want you to be mine. Forever."

Chase hugged her tightly. Mating with Sophie would be a dream come true, but still. Had he heard her right?

"Mating means...um... It requires..."

"A bite?" Sophie finally interjected in a low whisper that sounded shy and lusty at the same time.

Chase's jaw dropped. "You know about the bite?"

She laughed. "Anjali and Hailey came over two days ago while you were asleep and explained a few things to me."

He swallowed hard. Wow. He'd been meaning to thank the women of Koakea for all their help, but now he owed them even more.

"What exactly did they explain?"

Sophie leaned in close and whispered in his ear, "Everything."

He didn't know if she intended those words to arouse all the pent-up need in him, but they sure did. At the same time, he was stunned. The other women had explained mating to Sophie? He'd spent the last few days floating in and out of sleep, but now that he thought of it, he did have a vague memory of naughty giggles coming from the direction of the porch.

"Everything?" His voice was low, gritty, and full of desire.

"Everything." Sophie's lips brushed his ear, and she nestled closer, her hips right up against his growing erection. "They told me how good it feels. And that I get to bite you back — when I'm ready, I mean."

She nuzzled him, and he nuzzled back, high on her words. He ran his hands down her sides, teasing the edge of her breasts.

"You want that — the mating bite?" he triple-checked.

"I want it more than anything." Sophie nibbled his ear.

"You know it will bind us together forever. Really forever — more than any vows or marriage certificates could ever do. We'll be together for the rest of our lives and forever after, too."

She cupped his cheeks in both hands. "I do." Then she grinned. "You get it? I do?"

He laughed and smoothed her hair back, mainly to keep his hands from wandering too far south.

"It will make you a wolf shifter. Did the others explain that too?"

Sophie's throat bobbed, but she nodded firmly. "They explained that it can be dangerous for human males to turn shifter, but that it's easy for women to do."

Chase nodded. Men's bodies fought the change, and few survived the experience. Women, on the other hand, took to the inner changes more naturally.

Sophie's eyes took on a faraway look. "Anjali told me how great it feels — like the best yoga ever, with her joints going all limber. Hailey talked about feeling strong." She flashed a sad smile. "I figure I could use some of that."

He shook his head. "You already proved how strong you were, out by the blowhole."

She pursed her lips then went on. "Jenna told me about all the sights and smells — they all agreed on that. How good it feels. How natural. How in touch with the earth." Then she drew in a deep breath. "They said shifting was a gift."

Chase closed his eyes, thinking it over. He'd always taken his shifting ability for granted. But the others were right. It was a gift. One he couldn't wait to share with his mate.

So what are you waiting for? his wolf growled.

Still, Chase forced himself to ask one more time. "You're really okay with it?"

She bit her lip. "Honestly, I'm a little scared. But I'm... well... " She blushed harder. "I'm curious too."

For the next few seconds, they stared at each other. Then they kissed. Hard. Harder... Sophie hooked her leg around his, making her need clear, and when her hand brushed his cock, he nearly howled.

But Coco and Boris looked up, sniffing the lust-laced air, and Chase frowned. There was nothing he wanted more than to make Sophie his mate, but he'd prefer not to share the intimate moment with his new buddies.

"Hang on," he whispered, pulling Sophie to her feet.

The dogs scattered — except Darcy who glanced up from his comfortable pillow with a look that said, *What, again?*

Chase didn't stop to correct him. Yes, he and Sophie were going to make love again. But it would be like nothing they'd ever experienced before, and he knew it. Luckily, they were already naked, so all they needed was a little space.

"Up here," he urged Sophie, steering her toward the loft.

She stifled a giggle. "Good idea."

The dogs watched them climb the ladder, looking forlorn. But Chase was not about to feel guilty about finding privacy for the most important moment of his life.

Sophie didn't seem to mind either. In fact, she scaled the steep stairs faster than he'd ever seen her, and when she reached the top, she turned to face him.

"This is all new to me, but it feels like I've been waiting for this my whole life," she whispered, welcoming him into her arms.

Chase wished he could reply with a slick line, but he was too busy kissing her and lowering her to the mattress. Within seconds, they were wrapped around each other and panting with need.

"So good," Sophie murmured, tilting her head to the side.

He nearly moaned when he nipped her neck. An insatiable ache built inside him, making him nip harder. His canines started to extend, which Sophie had to feel, but she didn't protest.

"Yes. . ." she whispered, arching under him.

Her nipples went hard and high under his hands, and when he reached lower, touching her core, she moaned.

"More. . ."

Sophie started rocking against his hand, and he couldn't stop exploring her neck. Sniffing and nipping, seeking out the right spot to bite. The world around him faded away until all he could see, smell, or feel was Sophie. He suckled at a spot where her pulse beat closest to the surface.

There, his wolf howled. *Right there.*

Throughout his life, he'd thought about mating in an abstract way, and the bite seemed like the hardest, most dangerous part. But now that he had arrived at the moment, instinct guided him, and it felt simple. All he had to do was slide his teeth in gently, and Sophie would be his.

"Yes," she hissed, bucking against his body.

Everything felt perfect, except for one little detail that nagged at him. He raked his mind for what that might be.

Bite her. Fill her, his wolf chanted. *Make her ours.*

He closed his eyes, tapping into his deepest shifter instincts. What was missing? What was he doing wrong?

"Chase," Sophie moaned, going slick around the fingers he swept inside her.

She twisted slightly, and just like that, he knew what he needed.

"Turn," he murmured, guiding her into a roll. "Turn."

For the briefest of seconds, Sophie looked at him in surprise. Then her eyes sparkled, and she rolled, coming to her hands and knees.

Now, his wolf growled. *Now.*

He kneeled behind her and gripped her hips. He was on fire. Blinded. Hungry like never before.

So, take her, a deep voice rumbled in his mind.

They didn't have a condom, but they didn't need one. Not if they were going to be mates.

Sophie looked back at him over her shoulder with dark, lusty eyes. *Take me,* her body all but screamed.

The second Chase slid in, light exploded before his eyes.

Yes, his wolf panted.

"Yes," Sophie cried, pushing back.

He pulled her hips back, keeping her close, and thrust deeper. Harder. Nearly howling like the voice in his mind.

Take her. . .

He raked his teeth over her neck while rocking into her. The sex was rough, raw, and wild, but somehow, he needed it this way. Sophie seemed to as well, because she braced herself and pushed back, welcoming his thrusts.

"Chase. . ." she moaned as he homed in on the correct spot on her neck.

His senses piqued, and he swore he could hear the blood rush under her skin. Under his teeth, in fact, as he rested them on her hot flesh, making sure he had it right. Then he rocked harder, bringing Sophie to the very edge of ecstasy. And when she cried out and clenched around him—

Now, instinct cried.

He plunged his teeth deep. A white, searing heat ripped through his body. His cock pulsed, and he emptied inside her, climaxing at the same moment she did. When he pushed his teeth a tiny bit deeper, she moaned in ecstasy.

So good... He swore he heard her voice in his mind.

Deeper, his wolf insisted.

He sank his teeth deeper, covering the area with his lips. Holding on while the taste of her swirled over his tongue. Sophie danced under him as his shifter essence traveled through her veins.

Yes, she cried. *Yes...*

Every muscle in his body stiffened as he held on to the bite, then finally released it with a gasp. Panting hard, he smoothed a hand over her neck. Not a drop of blood blemished her silky skin, and the puncture marks instantly sealed over. Sophie cooed and murmured, barely seeming to notice.

"Oh yes..." She shuddered in an aftershock then slowly settled in his arms.

Chase's racing heart slowed down gradually. For the past weeks, he'd been afraid to get close to Sophie, fearful that his wolf would get out of control. But it turned out that getting a little wild was exactly what they needed to find real peace.

The road to that peace was littered with emotions, though, and they all seemed to gang up on him at the same time. Chase had never cried in his life. Not in his moments of greatest sorrow, nor the best moments of his life. But now...

He swallowed away the lump in his throat as a couple of tears slipped out. All his life, something had been missing. For all those years, he'd never really fit in. But now, all that washed away, and he felt utterly, perfectly, sinfully content.

"Sophie," he whispered, holding her close as he lowered himself to the mattress, completely spent.

He couldn't summon any words other than her name, but he could feel his thoughts rush into her mind, telling her just how good he felt. Did she feel that good too?

"Yes," she whispered, melting in his arms. "Yes, I do."

Chapter Eighteen

Sophie smoothed her hands over her shirt and checked her appearance for the third time. Her French braid looked fine, but her hands wouldn't stop skittering nervously over her clothes. When she caught herself sniffing the air, she chuckled.

"What?" Chase asked, coming up beside her. The moment he touched her shoulder, her jumpy nerves eased.

"Look at me, sniffing the air. Soon, I'll be howling to the moon."

She hadn't shifted yet, but she'd felt a change the moment Chase had bitten her. That had been three days ago, and she was still tingling from the high. Of course, they had been shagging wildly at all times of day — and night — ever since.

"Howling to the moon with me," Chase murmured, looking pleased.

The notion made her blood race. But then she wrinkled her nose and frowned.

"Yikes. We smell like sex."

"We smell like mates," Chase corrected, nuzzling her shoulder.

That only heightened the lusty scent in the air, because the slightest touch from her mate turned her on. That was another side effect of the change unfolding within her — the constant craving for her mate. Of course, she'd been wild about Chase from the start, but that need had intensified. How she'd resisted the urge to hop into bed with him from the very beginning, she had no clue.

But sadly, now was not the time. The sun was dipping toward the horizon, bringing another day to a close. A day she'd be happy to end in her mate's arms, but they had a meeting to attend first.

"Anyway," Chase added. "I think you smell good."

"*You* do. But everyone else..."

He shook his head. "Hey, we're shifters. No one will judge. Everyone is happy for you. For us, I mean."

He hugged her, and she closed her eyes in another of those *Pinch me, I'm dreaming* moments she'd experienced over the past few days. Then she pulled away, because her hands were already sliding down Chase's perfect ass, which would only get her sidetracked again.

"Okay, then. Meeting, here we come."

"Right." Chase nodded and moved aside to crouch beside Darcy. "Ready to take over here, Lieutenant?"

The dog wagged his tail, and Sophie beamed at the sight. Finally, her little warrior had accepted Chase as one of the good guys. Darcy had recovered enough to manage brief walks outside, but mostly he'd been lying on that pillow. They'd caught him dragging it to the front door a day earlier — the better to guard the house from, Sophie supposed. Not that he was in any shape to guard anything yet, but he would be back on his feet soon.

"Good boy," she said, petting him. Her brave little Darcy. "Will you guard our home for us?"

Darcy wagged his tail, and she smiled. She wasn't the only one who loved their new digs. The dogs had settled in quickly, prancing over the lawn and exploring the grounds. But even when Darcy was fully healed, Sophie had the feeling he would stick close to the house, guarding his home.

Home. She sighed. It had been ages since she'd truly been able to call a place that. Now, a feeling of contentment like none she'd ever known settled into her bones.

"Home is where the heart is," she murmured to herself, echoing her aunt's words. Then she smiled and remembered the punchline. *Being in Maui doesn't hurt either.*

She stood, sniffing the air wafting through the front door. The aroma of tropical flowers, the distant roll of waves over the shore. The musky scent of the woods, higher up along the slopes.

Home, a scratchy voice whispered in her mind.

The voice of her inner wolf was growing ever clearer. That thrilled and comforted her at the same time. Her step uncle Mike had died horribly because he'd resisted the beast emerging within him, but she had accepted hers from the very start.

Maybe Chase was right. Every human had a hidden, animal side, but she was more in touch with hers than most people were.

"Okay, then. You're in charge," Chase told Darcy. Then he took Sophie's hand and led her toward the main house.

She left Darcy with a last *Good boy,* which made him straighten with pride. Chase had been right about that as well. Every dog had one thing that made them tick, and for Darcy, that was all about earning her praise.

Coco and Boris were the same; they looked to Chase for approval and treated him like a god. On the whole, though, they were more simple, fun-loving souls than Darcy, and they loved chasing each other through the underbrush as Sophie and Chase walked along.

The blustery weather had come and gone, leaving Maui as lush and beautiful as ever. The light of the setting sun glinted off Sophie's locket and made the slopes of the plantation turn gold.

"All right, guys. Settle down," she called as they approached the main house.

They did no such thing, but the second Chase grunted a single syllable, they fell back to his heels.

"Yay! They're here!" a boy cried.

Joey, Cynthia's son, came hurtling down the porch stairs, heading straight for the dogs. Within seconds, he was chasing Coco in circles and having a great time. Keiki, the calico cat from the neighboring estate, stood on the stairs hissing at Boris. The greyhound stuck his tail between his legs and retreated behind Chase.

Chase chuckled and whispered to the dog, "Nothing to be ashamed of, man. That cat has the heart of a tiger."

Keiki stuck her nose up and turned to the adults on the porch with a look that said, *Who shall I allow to pet me next?* She settled for Dell and started purring under his hand.

"Come on, Boris," Joey squeaked. "We're playing tag!"

"Joey, sweetie, don't be too wild," Cynthia called.

Sophie smiled. If anyone had ever tried telling her the boy who played with her dogs was a dragon shifter, she never would have believed it. Now, she knew enough about shifters not to be alarmed. Joey wouldn't actually shift until he reached adolescence, for one thing, and he was really sweet, for another. She had no doubt dragons could be fierce as anything, but Cynthia had only been incredibly kind and welcoming.

She's got a soft spot for Chase, Anjali had explained.

Yeah, Dell had added. *Her only soft spot.*

Hailey had laughed at that. *Everyone has a soft spot for Chase.*

That was evident as Sophie and Chase came up the stairs, hand in hand. Everyone waved and called out fondly.

"Chase! Sophie!"

"Good to see you!"

"Yeah — finally," Dell quipped, winking at them while making his baby daughter wave.

Sophie blushed. Yes, they had spent most of the past three days making love in Chase's house. But as Chase had promised, no one teased. More than anything else, everyone was happy for them. Happy — and reliving their own first days together, Sophie guessed as the couples exchanged knowing glances.

Chase was the subject of much back-slapping from the guys, while Sophie was hugged by the women. It was like coming home to a warm, loving family after a long time away. She even choked up a little until Chase looped an arm over her shoulders and shot her a *Told you so* grin.

Sophie placed a hand on her locket. Koakea was so full of love. No wonder she felt so at home.

Still, she felt something special binding her to the other women there. A faint feeling she couldn't exactly place. Something beyond the fact that they'd all been through similar struggles in the course of finding their destined mates. Sophie looked around, wondering what could account for that.

She turned and saw Cynthia watching her — no, wait. Looking at her locket? A split second later, Cynthia jerked her gaze away. Sophie pursed her lips. Had that been a look of concern, or was she imagining things?

"Well, everyone, let's get started," Cynthia announced.

Everyone moved to their places around the table. A sense of anticipation filled the air that had little to do with the drinks and hors d'oeuvres that had been set out.

"Yes," Connor, Chase's oldest brother, agreed. "Time to get started."

Sophie looked around. It was all so obvious now — the family ties, the subtle shifter hierarchy. Connor and Cynthia were co-alphas of their pack. The others all filled their own special roles while supporting their leaders, with everyone pulling together for the common good. In some ways, it resembled the clan Sophie's stepfather had strived to create, with one major difference — this was a community based on love and trust, and that came shining through.

Her locket warmed, and again, she felt Cynthia's gaze. But Keiki drew her attention as she balanced daintily on the railing, brushing under pink bougainvillea that grew as high as the roof.

"So, do we get to toast these guys?" Dell asked.

"Not yet," Cynthia said.

"Aw, come on, Cynth," he protested.

"Cynthia," she sighed.

But Dell went on as if he hadn't heard. "We've only been waiting for these guys to get together for about..." He checked the clock on the wall. "Say, a few years."

"Six months," Tim corrected, rolling his bulging bear shoulders.

Sophie wasn't too good at reading Chase's mind yet, but at that moment, his thoughts came through loud and clear.

Six months, one week, two days, and nine hours, he sighed.

Her heart thumped a little harder at that reminder of how long they'd pined for each other.

Anjali poked Dell. "Would you give them a break? Some things take time."

Dell gave an exaggerated sigh. "Some things take *forever*. Like this guy." He thumped Chase on the shoulder. "And dinner. When are we going to eat? Quinn and I spent ages making all this great food, and here we are, sitting around. Right, sweetie?" He tickled the baby in his lap.

Sophie warmed. That was one thing she loved about Chase's extended family — the humor. The banter. The give-and-take. The love that came shining through every word, glance, and gesture.

Baby Quinn squirmed, pointing to Joey and the dogs. "Do. Do."

"Doggies," Dell said in baby talk as he stood. "Call me when you get to the food, guys. Quinn and I are going to have some fun."

And off he went, charging down to the lawn like an overgrown kid. Anjali watched them go with a twinkle in her eye, and Sophie couldn't help wishing that might be her someday — watching her own mate play lovingly with their own kids.

She glanced at Chase and immediately blushed. Everything in its time, right?

"A toast is definitely in order." Cynthia smiled. "But we have a few things to go over first."

"Right," Connor agreed. "Just to make sure we're all on the same page when it comes to this case. Like David, for starters."

Sophie frowned and looked at her hands. David's body had turned up after an extensive search of the coast, and police had called the death an accident. Sophie didn't know what Connor and the others had done with the bodies of the shifters, and she didn't care. She wanted to look into the future, not into the past.

"Sorry to bring it up," Connor added quickly. "But we've found evidence that may connect David to an...er..."

"Associate of ours," Cynthia filled in when he searched for words.

Connor nodded. "And we need to follow up on that."

Sophie bobbed her head. She owed these shifters her life. Anything they needed to know, she'd tell them. So she went through it all from the beginning — why she'd left home and how David had followed her, first from Maine to Vermont, and eventually, to Maui.

"When he showed up here, I thought he was after me," she said. "But then he started asking about my aunt's money..."

When she trailed off there, Hailey spoke up in a hushed voice. "Camille Carmichael. Her landscape photography is just stunning. I would have loved to have met her."

A lump rose in Sophie's throat. Her aunt would have liked Hailey too.

Anjali looked grim. "I can't believe anyone would want to murder a girl they grew up with for money."

Sophie made a face. She couldn't believe it either.

"Look, I hate to ask," Connor went on. "But how much was it?"

Chase put up a hand as if his brother had crossed an imaginary line, but Cynthia spoke first.

"Just bear with us for a moment, please. We know David wanted to use that money to expand the militia's activities. What we're trying to understand is whether there was even more on the line than that."

Sophie fiddled with the tablecloth. She could scarcely imagine something worse than what David had been plotting. Was there really another element to his attempts on her life?

"Two-point-five million dollars," she whispered, looking at Chase.

Yes, she'd finally done it. A few days earlier, she'd met with her aunt's lawyer and learned all the details of the money entrusted to her. Two-point-five million dollars was more than she would have ever known what to do with, but neither Connor nor Cynthia looked impressed.

"That's it?" Connor demanded.

Sophie blinked. "I beg your pardon?"

Chase growled under his breath. "Yeah. I beg your pardon?"

Connor stuck his hands up. "Sorry. I didn't mean it that way. But—"

Tim cut him off. "I'd say that's plenty of money. Enough to save an entire wolf pack."

Sophie beamed. Her aunt's last wish had been for Sophie to find a good cause to put her money toward, and thanks to Chase and Tim, Sophie had done just that.

Hailey patted Tim's broad back, beaming with pride. "I'm so glad that worked out."

Sophie couldn't agree more. She'd been dismayed to hear about the danger to Chase's home pack. But Tim's bear shifter friends had reported back with good — and bad — news. The bad news was that the wolf pack's natural territory covered a huge plot of private property which was up for sale. Worse, David's militia buddies had been in the area, looking for a secluded property on which to establish a new base — and they'd been poaching on the side for kicks. That sickened Sophie, but the good news was, the land was for sale, and her aunt's money was just enough to seal the deal.

"Have the lawyers finished all the paperwork?" Jenna asked eagerly.

Sophie shook her head. "It will take some time, but everything looks good."

Chase covered her hand with both of his, letting her know how much that meant to him. Tim shot Sophie a grateful look too. The land was being put into a trust, and Tim's bear shifter friends had happily agreed to watch over that property in addition to their own.

"A win-win for everyone." Hailey's voice filled with pride.

"No one can harm them now," Sophie whispered, kissing Chase's hand.

"No one," he echoed, looking at her with eyes that glowed with gratitude.

Sophie closed her eyes. She'd never wanted any money for herself, and she was sure her aunt would have loved the idea. Her aunt had also left her the bungalow, and that meant more to Sophie than all the money in the world. It would be a great place for her and Chase to use on weekends or if they ever wanted to stay over close to town. Her primary home, though, would be Chase's place.

Forever, her inner wolf hummed happily.

The sea breeze wafted over the porch, stirring the table-cloth, but no one made a move toward the food. Dell came back up the stairs with Quinn, and even he didn't utter a word.

Connor spoke up solemnly. "We're still trying to figure out one thing. The shifters that turned up to help David..."

Sophie's mood ebbed again. David's obsession with shifters had been his downfall, just like her stepfather and her stepuncle before him.

Tim looked grim. "Something tells me you have a theory about them too."

Connor glanced at Cynthia, who nodded for him to go on.

"I have more than a theory. Chase said they mentioned Moira, and our sources have just come through with new in-formation."

Everyone leaned forward, but Sophie shrank back. Chase had told her about Moira — a bitter, conniving dragon shifter and mortal enemy of the shifters of Koakea and Koa Point.

Hailey and Anjali exchanged worried glances. Chase, Tim, and Dell looked downright murderous. Cynthia sat very still, her face a mask.

"Moira is mixed up in this? Why? How?" Dell asked.

Tim's brow furrowed deeply. "What is Moira after now?"

"What is Moira always after?" Connor said bitterly. "Us. Trouble. That about sums it up."

"But what does that have to do with David?" Chase asked.

"Yeah," Tim demanded. "Two million dollars is petty cash to Moira. Why would she care about him?"

Connor scratched his chin. "I wondered the same thing. It makes sense for David to have caught Moira's attention with his interest in shifters, but what would be in it for her?"

"There's always something in it for her," Cynthia muttered.

Sophie tried not to stare. Just how far back did Cynthia and Moira go?

"From what we can gather, Moira and David struck a deal," Connor explained. "Moira promised David she'd help him turn shifter—"

Sophie couldn't help butting in there. "I thought you said that didn't work for men."

Cynthia made a face. "It rarely does, but that wouldn't stop Moira from making another false promise."

Sophie closed her eyes. It had been bad enough to deal with David, but Moira sounded like a whole different level of dangerous.

"I don't get it," Anjali chipped in. "Moira is rich. She's surrounded herself with top shifter bodyguards, and she's expanding her business empire. What could she possibly need David for?"

Connor uttered one syllable, and everyone went deadly silent.

"Us."

Sophie looked around the people gathered there on the porch. Each was a powerful shifter in his or her own right, yet each looked troubled.

"What do you mean, us?" Tim asked.

"David was Moira's means to getting at Sophie, and Sophie was her means of getting at us."

Sophie's jaw dropped, and the blood drained out of her cheeks. She'd sooner die than bring trouble to Chase's family. What had she done?

"But... But..." she stammered, feeling sick.

"It's not your fault," Cynthia assured her. "This is classic Moira."

"Over a year ago, Moira came here in person in an attempt to kill Silas." Connor jerked his thumb north, to the neighboring estate where Silas lived.

Sophie's mind raced. Silas was the owner of both properties, and a dragon shifter. Chase had explained as much when he'd gone over the local who's who of shifters.

"Silas and his mate Cassandra were able to repel the attack," Connor said. "But Moira has been keeping tabs on us

ever since. Looking for a way to attack — or at least to disrupt
— our lives."

Tim rubbed his chin. "So she would have known about
Chase and Sophie."

Sophie's cheeks turned crimson. Had the whole world followed her blossoming romance?

Connor shot her an apologetic look. "Hey, we were rooting
for you guys. But Moira would have seen it as an opportunity.
You know, going after the weak link."

Chase growled. "Weak link?"

"We have no weak link," Tim grunted.

"Especially not Sophie," Jenna snorted.

Connor stuck his hands up. "That's what Moira would
think, not me. She probably figured an attack on Sophie would
draw Chase's attention away. Theoretically, that would weaken
our defenses—"

Chase growled. "Would not."

Connor made a face. "I said theoretically, all right? And,
hey. I'll admit to being a little distracted when my mate was
in danger."

Dell rolled his eyes. "A little distracted?"

Connor shot him one of those alpha warning looks Sophie
was beginning to recognize. "Anyway, that's about the gist of
it. David was just another pawn in one of Moira's games. She
had no intention of helping him turn shifter."

Sophie's stomach turned. She'd left home wishing never to
see David again, but she'd never wished him dead.

Dell sat back, shaking his head. "That's so fucked up, it
fits Moira perfectly." Anjali shot him a sharp look, and he
covered baby Quinn's ears. "Sorry, honey. But it's true."

"It is true," Anjali sighed.

Everyone went quiet for a time, mulling over the news.
Sophie took several deep breaths, taking solace from Chase's
steady presence. He credited destiny with bringing them together, and she believed it. But, boy. Destiny certainly had a
way of messing with people's lives.

Chase shook his head, reading her thoughts. *David's death
isn't your fault,* he whispered into her mind. *Besides, I have*

185

a feeling that wasn't all destiny. Sometimes, people make bad choices, and destiny lets them get what they deserve.

Sophie touched her locket. There'd been so many times she'd felt it guiding her. Was that destiny, or was it something else? Her eyes strayed to the row of palms swaying down by the shore and then across the glittering sea.

"It's true," Cynthia said in summary, and Sophie expected her to move on to something else. But Cynthia's expression remained serious, and her eyes landed right on Sophie's locket. "But I wonder whether Moira had her sights on yet another prize."

Five seconds ticked by, and then another five. Sophie was struck by the urge to hide her locket, but she forced herself to cup it in her hand instead.

"This?" she asked in a shaky voice.

Cynthia nodded. "That."

"But it's just a locket," Sophie protested.

Cynthia arched one thin eyebrow. "Is it?"

Chapter Nineteen

Sophie looked around, stunned. Chase looked ready to growl at Cynthia, but his face showed deep concern.

"What do you mean?" Sophie asked, turning the heart-shaped locket over a few times to show how ordinary it was. As a sentimental keepsake, the locket was invaluable, but it wasn't special in any other sense.

Other than the sea breeze stirring the bougainvillea that grew along the porch, nothing moved, and no one said a word. It was Cynthia who finally jutted her chin toward the locket and spoke.

"I suspect Moira may have wanted David to procure it for her. May I ask what's inside?"

Sophie undid the clasp to show how harmless its contents were. "It's nothing, really. Just this."

She laughed as she said it, then froze. Why was everyone staring?

"Whoa," Connor muttered, taken aback.

"Wow." Hailey's eyebrows flew up.

"Ho-ly shit," Dell said, drawing out the syllables.

Sophie turned to Chase, but his jaw was hanging open too.

What was so special about a single pearl? Sophie frowned and hurried to explain.

"It's not valuable or anything." She gestured at the white ball cushioned in a tiny scrap of silk. "At least, not in terms of money."

Her words fell on deaf ears, because everyone continued to gawk.

"Where did you get that?" Cynthia's voice was tight.

Sophie closed and opened the locket a few times in a losing battle to convince everyone it was nothing special. Or was it? She studied it closely. There was no inscription, just the pearl, but her aunt had always had a special affinity for the locket. It might as well have been a holy relic, the way she had talked about it.

Trust this. Trust yourself. It will help you find love.

A little shiver went down Sophie's spine, but she shook it off. Her aunt had believed in a lot of kooky things. That didn't mean they were all true, right?

"My aunt gave it to me," she said, summing up so much in a few words. Her aunt had been dying at the time, but she'd seemed at peace. That was how deep her trust in love and the beauty of the universe ran.

"And where did your aunt get it?" Cynthia asked with barely hidden urgency.

"From her partner — the man she fell in love with and moved to Maui for, years ago. Lionel Mahelona."

"The artist?" Hailey exclaimed.

Sophie nodded. "Lionel was a painter, and my aunt was a photographer. She'd only planned to visit Maui for a short time to shoot landscapes, but then she met Lionel, and she never left."

"Sounds like quite the love story," Hailey murmured.

Sophie nodded. "It was. They never spent a day apart. When Lionel died two years ago, my aunt said part of her died too." Then she inhaled, backing up. "Neither had really had much success before they met, but when they got together, both their careers took off." She smiled faintly. "But money and attention weren't important to them. All my aunt really ever valued was love. She said she and Lionel were soul mates."

"Destiny," Hailey whispered, looking deep into Tim's eyes.

Sophie turned the locket over. She'd been so preoccupied, she hadn't given the locket or pearl much thought.

"Do you think it's significant somehow?" she asked Cynthia.

Cynthia's lips pinched, and Sophie had the distinct impression she'd made a huge understatement

"Yes," Cynthia whispered. "I believe it is."

Sophie wasn't sure what to expect next, but when Cynthia turned to the other women, she was really confused.

"Show her," Cynthia bid the others. "Please."

Sophie looked around. Show her what?

Jenna looked at Connor then reached into her pocket. Sophie's jaw hung open when Jenna pulled out a beautiful black pearl with a golden tint. Hailey followed by taking out a pink pearl of her own. Then Anjali pulled a necklace from under her shirt, displaying a brown pearl.

Sophie stared at each of those three pearls, then at the one in her hand. The others were all exotic colors, while hers was a pure, eggshell white. It usually looked dull, with a matte finish. But now, her pearl came alive with light, almost glowing from the inside.

"One of the pearls of desire," Anjali whispered.

The pearls of what? Sophie nearly choked on her own breath.

The other pearls were glowing as well — practically winking at each other, given the way sunlight bounced from one to the other. But they were under the shade of the porch, so it couldn't have been the sun.

"Wow," Jenna breathed. "Another one."

Chase looked absolutely speechless.

"Another one?" Sophie stammered.

"Another of the pearls of desire," Cynthia said.

Chase squeezed her hand, assuring her that wasn't a bad thing.

"It's a legend," he said, as hoarse as he'd been those first few days after the fight.

"Not just a legend," Anjali said firmly.

Sophie stared at Anjali's pearl, speechless.

"Does it get warm?" Jenna asked.

Just when Sophie's jaw had finally felt realigned, it fell open again.

"Well, yes. But that's just..."

Jenna's look said that wasn't *just* anything.

"Does it pep you up when you feel down?" Hailey asked. "I know that sounds crazy, but I mean it. Mine does. All those times I felt alone..."

She laced her fingers through Tim's and shot him a grateful look that said those days were long gone.

"Does it give you strength?" Anjali asked.

Sophie touched the pearl with one finger. "Sometimes, just having it makes me feel... braver than I would otherwise." She looked up, sure they would mock her for that, but every woman nodded as if she knew exactly how Sophie felt. Slowly, she went on. "And in the fight..."

She trailed off. That had to be her imagination twisting her memories, right? But those rocks she'd thrown hadn't just pestered the grizzly — they'd genuinely interfered with the beast. And the way she'd been able to shove David in that make-or-break moment...

"Sophie's no pushover," Chase said, looping an arm over her shoulders.

She could have kissed him for having such faith — more than she ever had in herself. But the more she thought about it, the more she felt something else had been involved.

Anjali smiled. "Of course, Sophie is no pushover. But even the best of us could use a boost at the worst of times."

She spoke as if she knew just how it felt to stare down death and survive, and Sophie nodded. "It was like that. Exactly the way you describe."

"Not just a legend." Jenna nodded firmly.

Sophie put the locket in one hand and the pearl in the other, and pursed her lips. "Wow."

"Do you feel it?" Anjali asked with shining eyes.

Sophie raised the hand holding the pearl. "I always thought it was just the locket reflecting my body heat. I never thought it was the pearl." Then she looked up. "What does the legend say?"

Cynthia stood wordlessly and stepped into the house, while the other women looked at each other, deciding who would speak first.

"Nanalani," Chase whispered in the silence that ensued.

Sophie tilted her head at him. Nana-what?

Jenna nodded and took over from there. "It's a Hawaiian legend — that of Nanalani, daughter of the shark king."

Sophie's breath caught in her throat. She'd only just come around to the idea of wolf, bear, and lion shifters. Dragons were still a little scary, but yikes — sharks, too?

Cynthia returned with a heavy, leather-bound book that looked centuries old, and Connor cleared some space on the table.

"So much for dinner," Dell sighed.

Anjali shushed him with a firm look.

Cynthia leafed through a few pages and then turned the book around so Sophie could see. Most of the page was filled with swirly, decorative script, but the bottom was illustrated with a scene of a tropical island.

"Is that Maui?" Sophie whispered, studying the waterfall, craggy mountains, and golden strips of sand.

Cynthia nodded. "We think so. Somewhere in Hawaii, for sure."

Sophie leaned closer to examine the rest. A woman stood waist-deep in the ocean, unconcerned by the shark circling nearby. Her focus lay entirely on the seashell cupped in her hands — a seashell full of pearls.

"Nanalani was terrified that her shark side might emerge and hurt her human friends," Jenna explained. "So she kept away, exiling herself to a cave."

Sophie's heart ached. Yeah, she could identify with that. For years, she had been afraid to get close to anyone. Her crazy family had threatened her; what if they hurt her friends?

Jenna pointed to a passage in the text. "*In her loneliness and sorrow, Nanalani called forth the spirit of the sea. Together, they put a spell on her pearls — the pearls of desire. Her treasures allowed her to go safely forth as a woman and love a man she had admired from afar. Over the years, Nanalani had many lovers, though she never found her mate.*" Jenna looked up with shining eyes. "This is the key part. Ready?"

Sophie wasn't sure she was ready for anything, but when Chase gripped her hand, she nodded. With him, she could handle just about anything.

Jenna moved her finger along the next section of text. *"As time went on and her lovers passed away, Nanalani threw her pearls back into the sea, one by one. 'Now I am alone again,' she sighed to the god of the sea. 'I give you my pearls, not to keep, but to safeguard for another worthy lover who needs their power someday.'"* Jenna looked up and pointed at Sophie. "That's you."

Sophie's eyes went wide. "Me?"

"It was each of us, once upon a time," Anjali said.

When Anjali looked at Dell with eyes so full of love, Sophie could have sighed. But Chase was looking at her with exactly the same expression, and her soul soared. For years, she'd feared love was something she would only ever witness from the outside. But her turn had come at last.

Love will never, ever fade, a little voice whispered in her mind.

Chase nodded and kissed her hands. Had he heard that too?

Sophie closed her eyes a moment too late to catch the tear sliding down her cheek. She brushed it away, feeling silly. But a furtive glance showed her that the others looked a little teary-eyed as well — even those big, tough guys. Connor looked at Jenna like he was about to spout poetry, although he wasn't exactly the poetic type. Tim gazed at Hailey like she was his sun, his moon — his entire universe. Dell pulled Anjali close to form a little huddle around baby Quinn, and Cynthia. . .

Sophie bit her lip, because Cynthia faced the sea, alone. A lonely rock in a sea of happiness, a barren island of her own.

Sophie twisted her hands in her lap and leaned into Chase. She'd never felt so lucky in her life, but guilt gnawed at her. Didn't Cynthia deserve the same?

Then Sophie spotted Hailey glancing at Jenna and Anjali, who each gave a barely perceptible nod. They'd gone from *dizzy with love* to *determined* in the blink of an eye, and Sophie wondered why. Then it hit her. Those women had all gone out of their way to help her get together with Chase. Would they turn their matchmaking efforts to Cynthia next?

Sophie caught Hailey's eye and did her best to communicate, *Whatever you have planned, I'm in.*

"And you said your aunt got the pearl from her partner?" Cynthia asked, all business again.

Sophie rubbed her cheeks, trying to change gears. "Yes. From Lionel."

"An islander?" Cynthia leaned closer.

She nodded. "Yes. His roots on Maui went way back, and his nephews and nieces inherited his paintings and studio." Then she gasped. "Wait. Lionel painted pearls. Well, he painted a lot of island themes. But he always hid a pearl in a painting when he wanted to represent love."

"Did he ever mention the legend?" Cynthia asked.

Sophie shook her head. "No, but he did say some things were just for islanders to know. He was really nice about it, though." Her mind drifted off on memories. When she'd visited as a kid, Lionel had been friendly but busy with his art, and her aunt had mostly spoken to her about kid things.

She closed her eyes, aching at the loss of those two special people. "It really was true love," she whispered to no one in particular. Then she looked at Chase and took both his hands.

True love, he said. *Destiny.*

She rested her head against his. Her aunt had often said she didn't have a single regret, and Sophie could identify with that. Whether she got to live another ten, twenty, or fifty years with Chase, she'd bask in every moment of the love they shared.

The pearls glinted at each other from around the table. Cynthia wore a strand of pearls, and for a split second, Sophie thought one of them shone, too.

"Is that one of the pearls of desire?" she ventured.

Cynthia pinched her lips and touched her necklace. "Just the normal kind, I'm afraid. A gift from my mother."

"Oh," Sophie said, feeling stupid. But that one in the middle had really seemed to shine. She looked at the book, desperate to change the topic. "So, there are five?"

Jenna nodded. "Apparently. And between us, we have four."

Sophie looked around. Each pearl matched one in the illustration. Which left a blue-hued one, if the picture in the book held true.

"Wouldn't Moira love to get her hands on one," Dell mused. Then he smacked Chase on the back. "Good job keeping it away from her. You too, Sophie. Well done."

Chase looked as if he'd rather not think about it, but Sophie couldn't help asking, "What would Moira do if she had one?"

No one seemed eager to reply. Eventually, Connor spoke in a growl. "That's what we're worried about. Moira might try to twist the pearls' power."

"But desire..." Sophie blushed as heated images rushed through her mind.

Jenna flashed a quick smile. "It can mean that, for sure. But desire can be for lots of things."

"Like greed." Connor frowned. "Power."

Sophie's hand might have trembled if it weren't for Chase there with her. She didn't want to imagine what a vengeful dragon shifter might do in her quest for power.

"But there's good desire too," Dell pointed out. "Love. Lust. Right, honey?" he teased Anjali, who gave him one of her scolding looks.

"Let's call it passion, shall we?"

Dell grinned wickedly. "Passion. I like that."

"Commitment." Hailey locked eyes with Tim.

Yearning, Chase whispered into Sophie's mind.

She swallowed away her sorrow. That was all in her past. Now, all she felt was love.

"Joy," she replied.

"Undying love," Cynthia whispered, looking at the sunlight glinting over the Pacific. Sophie followed her eyes. All that space. All that emptiness.

Then she shook her head and corrected herself. The world was full of love and beauty, and someday, she'd help Cynthia see it too.

"Then there's this part," Jenna said, going back to the book. "*'And so it was that the pearls of desire — one for every kind of desire known to mankind — were lost, though legend claims they remain slumbering under the surface, waiting to be reawakened to inspire great acts of love again.'*"

"Amen," Dell said. "Let's hope love wins out in the end."

Sophie sure hoped so. And if there was any way she could help her friends obtain the last pearl, she would.

"You know what a white pearl signifies, don't you?" Cynthia asked, smiling again.

Sophie looked up, happy to change to a lighter topic. "I don't know much about pearls, to be honest."

Cynthia's smile stretched. "Maybe that's why it chose you. White is for innocence. Beauty. Purity."

Everyone nodded as if they agreed, and Sophie just about melted into her seat. Did they really mean her?

Chase kissed her. *Yep. They do.*

"And new beginnings," Cynthia added. "I'd say your pearl has found the right person, don't you agree?"

Sophie nodded, too choked up to speak. Now she knew why she felt so close to the other women and so at home in this place. The pearl had brought her to a perfect home.

Our home, Chase echoed in her mind.

Dell knocked on the table, getting everyone's attention. "I'd say that brings us to that toast — finally. Ready, guys?"

Everyone reached for their glasses and grinned.

"Hurry, sweetie," Cynthia called down to Joey, who rushed up and stood by her side with a *Star Wars* glass filled with juice.

"Yay, a toast," he cheered.

Cynthia beamed at her son and raised her glass. "To new beginnings."

"To Chase and Sophie," Anjali said, grinning.

"To love," Chase whispered, raising his glass too.

Sophie hurried to follow, and everyone clinked.

"To us," Dell added, setting off a second round of clinks. "I mean, all of us. I have to say, we make a pretty good team."

"That, we do," Connor agreed, and everyone cheered.

Sophie couldn't stop smiling over the next hour, as toasts turned to animated chatter and eventually to happy munches as they dug into the meal. Her first dinner as part of the Koakea family, and it was a memorable one. The stars came out one by one, and roars of laughter punctuated the chirp of crickets that filled the night. The ocean whispered over the shoreline not too far away, and the dogs sniffed around the yard, perfectly content. Joey was getting too big to cuddle in Cynthia's lap, but he did anyway, and baby Quinn yawned in her father's arms.

Sophie snuggled closer to Chase, soaking it all in. Home. Love. Beauty. How had she gotten so lucky?

Destiny, her inner wolf hummed.

She sighed. She could have stayed there forever if it weren't for one thing. Her wolf was starting to pace, restless in spite of it all.

What? Sophie wanted to demand. *What else could you possibly want?*

My mate, it replied in a lusty growl. *Want my mate.*

And just like that, the lazy feeling of contentment that Sophie had settled into became a burning need. She wiggled against Chase, whose hands slid over her legs, out of sight beneath the tablecloth. Apparently, his wolf had been talking to him in the same way.

She slid her leg over his, wondering if they could make a subtle exit. Luckily, Dell solved that problem for her.

"Well," he announced, standing so quickly, his chair screeched. "I think Quinn needs a bottle."

"She's sleeping," Cynthia pointed out dryly.

Anjali jumped up too, practically glued to Dell's side. "He means a diaper change."

"Quinn definitely needs a diaper change," Dell agreed, sliding his hand along Anjali's hip.

Jenna stood next, and her face was flushed. "Yeah, we have to go too. You know, to... uh... "

"Check the perimeter," Connor filled in.

His eyes roved over his mate's body, hinting at which *perimeter* he intended to check.

"Exactly." Jenna's eyes glowed with lust.

Hailey faked a yawn, and Tim helped her to her feet as if in no rush at all. His voice was a little strained, though. "Well, we'll be getting to bed, then."

"I bet you will." Cynthia sighed.

"Is it story time, Mommy?" Joey twisted in her lap.

Cynthia smiled. "I think it is, sweetie."

Chase stood, keeping Sophie nice and close, where she could feel every hard muscle of his body. "Do you want us to clean up?" he asked in a voice that prayed the answer would be *no*.

"We'll get it tomorrow," Cynthia said, waving a hand lazily.

"Wow," Dell called. "Was that really you, Cynth?"

"Goodnight, Mr. O'Roarke," she ordered.

Sophie smiled. For all the teasing, the love in this pack shone through. All kinds, from brotherly love to hard-earned respect and the love of devoted couples.

Don't forget lust, Chase whispered into her mind as he moved briskly toward the stairs.

Sophie giggled. So much for having a shy, retiring mate.

"I can't help it," he admitted, running a hand down her rear. "Not around you." Then Boris and Coco rushed over, nearly tripping him up, and he sighed. "You guys again."

Sophie laughed and inched closer to Chase's ear, pressing her chest against him so he wouldn't lose track of where they'd been.

No such danger, her wolf chuckled, making her rub against the hard area of his jeans.

"Good thing we have that loft," she said, sending lusty images into his mind as they walked.

Then a thought struck her, and she shot him a sidelong glance. "Wait a second. You said you built that loft months ago. Did you ever guess how handy it would be?"

Chase grinned and stopped to kiss her full on the lips. A long, hard kiss that promised a thorough follow-up once they got to bed.

"Like I said." He smiled. "It was destiny."

Epilogue

Two weeks later...

Chase padded toward the beach, sniffing the breeze. The earth was cool under his paws, and the scent of *pikake* filled his nose. The moonlight cast dancing shadows as palms undulated in the sea breeze.

"So many stars..." Sophie murmured as they walked. "It's beautiful."

He nodded and grinned up at her. Way up, because he was down on all fours in wolf form while Sophie walked alongside him. They headed down the long slope from the converted barn, past the vegetable garden he and Sophie had started to dig, and past Dell's creekside house, where everyone appeared fast asleep. The whole world seemed to slumber, giving him and Sophie all of Maui to enjoy on their own.

It had been two weeks since the mating bite, and Sophie hadn't shifted yet, but she'd had a lot of wolf dreams. Good dreams, thank goodness, which she woke from with wide, fascinated eyes.

"I felt it! I was running on all fours!" she'd announced once, breathless and thrilled.

He'd been thrilled too, seeing her get in tune with her animal side.

Another time, she'd dreamed of barking, and yet another, she'd dreamed about digging.

He'd laughed. "Digging for what?"

She'd shrugged. "I don't know. You know how dreams are. Everything seems important while you're dreaming, even if it's nothing. But it was so fun! All that dirt flying. Now I know why Boris does it."

They had a good laugh over that one, and the next day, Chase had gone out and had a good dig himself, like he used to as a pup. Front paws scooping, back legs just far enough apart to kick the dirt through. He'd made a mental note to teach her the joys of digging in shallow water someday, because splashing added to the fun.

He'd spent the entire next day grinning, he felt that good. For years, he'd painstakingly hidden his wolf side from the human world. It was strangely liberating to be able to share the joy of it all with Sophie — from the thrills to the quirky little things he'd never appreciated before. Like scratching an ear with his back foot. Turning three times before curling up to sleep. And best of all, doing a deep, doggie stretch before starting his day.

"No wonder they call it downward dog." Sophie had laughed, watching him do it.

For most of his life, he'd never quite fit in. Not in the wolf pack, not in the human world. An involuntary rebel, as his brothers had once joked. But now, he felt absolutely, positively content being himself. Truly at peace.

And Sophie, thank goodness, was the same way, despite all the changes she'd experienced. She seemed excited — even eager — to shift, and she had been hearing her inner wolf more and more clearly all the time. She'd even had dirty wolf dreams, as she'd admitted, blushing a deep crimson color.

Good ones, I hope? he'd asked.

She'd nodded quickly. *Amazing. I can't wait.*

Frankly, he couldn't wait for her to shift either. But on the other hand, he was pretty content as things were. Settling in to a new life with his mate, enjoying night walks like these — especially when Sophie rested her hand lightly on his back as she strode along at his side.

"Listen," she said, pointing to the left.

Her senses were growing more discerning, especially when it came to scent and sound.

Good one, he called into her mind as Buzz — their newest dog — came dashing out of the underbrush.

Sophie had spotted the skinny stray shivering under a park bench after a rainstorm. Neither the police nor the animal shelter had a matching report of a missing dog, so they'd taken in the mutt who was part corgi, part terrier, and part *nobody knows.*

"Your family is growing fast," Dell had commented.

Chase hadn't answered, lest he give anything away. He hoped to have lots of kids with Sophie someday, but for now. . . Well, dogs were fun too. His own little pack. And Sophie was right — the more love they shared, the more joy filled their days. Which shouldn't have been possible, but he was learning that happiness knew no bounds, as Buzz demonstrated by tearing around them in three hyper circles, then dashing away again. The mutt had been left locked indoors for most of the day before his owner abandoned him. At least, that was what they'd gathered from the scattered memories that flitted through the dog's mind. Lately, though, Buzz had nothing but good things to report.

Wow, wow, wow, he yipped to the other dogs. *Smelly bear poop over there!*

And, *zoom!* Off they went — all four dogs — to investigate, leaving Chase and Sophie in peace. Even Darcy scampered after them, entrusting his nice lady to Chase. Sophie and Chase continued toward the beach, and when they turned the last corner of the twisting path, Sophie sighed at the view.

"So beautiful."

Chase wagged his tail so hard, it swatted her legs, but she didn't seem to mind. It really was beautiful. The nearly full moon was close to setting, with a few hours to go until sunrise. They were awake that early because Sophie had been too restless to sleep.

"All my life, I missed seeing things like this," she whispered, looking up at a sky alive with stars, all twinkling merrily.

Chase walked with her to the waterline and thumped his tail in agreement. Most humans stuck to regular daylight hours, and that was a crying shame. How many moonrises and moon-

201

sets did the average human see in their lifetime? How many shooting stars?

Sophie sat in the sand, and he sat next to her, keeping her side warm with his huge wolf body. She looped an arm over his back and absently petted his ears, making him hum with pleasure as they looked up at the Milky Way.

"Someday, when I can shift..." she murmured.

Chase nuzzled her, trying to look mournful when he was secretly delighted at her impatience.

Take all the time you need, he said. *I'll always love you, even if you never shifted at all — but I know you will soon,* he hastened to add when she shot him a worried glance.

"I feel ready." She sighed and picked up a handful of sand then let the grains pour slowly between her fingers like an hourglass. "But somehow, nothing is happening."

He didn't know what to say, having never been in that position, but he nuzzled her thoroughly, and that seemed to help. Then he pushed his head back and let out a long, warbly call, warming up his voice.

Sophie smiled beside him. "I love listening to you sing."

Then she sat in silence as if attending the performance of a fancy orchestra. And in a way, that fit. The water lapping at the shoreline created a steady undertone, and chirping crickets played a quick tune. Palm fronds swished like so many string instruments, leaving just one thing missing. A wolf call.

Chase closed his eyes, took a deep breath, and howled, holding the note as long as he could. *Arooooo....*

All that sound resonating in his chest felt good, so he did it again. He made sure the notes were slow and ponderous, just the way he'd been taught as a pup. Back then, he'd been envious of the way the oldest, most grizzled wolves were able to stretch out their howls, letting them echo off the hills. Now, he was pretty good at it himself, if not quite the experts they were.

He swallowed one note, smiling to himself. Someday he'd be an old, grizzled wolf with so many memories to look back on — especially good ones.

Then he started a new note, and it was the best yet — nice, round, and full-bodied, if a sound could be called such a thing. The longer he howled, the more satisfied he felt, and he could sense Sophie sigh in contentment too.

The first time she'd listened to him howl, her eyes had filled with tears. "It sounds so sad."

He'd shifted back to human form to explain. "Wolf howls are like ballads — there's always something sad in them. But that's only to get started. Then you sing about all the good stuff."

"Like what?" she'd asked, eager, as always, to learn.

"Like you."

That made her smile, and him, too.

Since then, he'd gone out howling regularly, just for the joy of it. Like at that very moment — celebrating the close of another great day with Sophie and celebrating the beginning of a new one, with many more ahead.

The row of cliffs where Connor and Jenna had their dragon lair stood just south of the beach, absorbing most of the sound, so he didn't have to fear any neighbors overhearing. And, anyway, their nearest neighbors were the shifters of Koa Point, who emitted their fair share of howling, yowling, and feline calls.

So he sang on and on, happier than he'd ever been, dreaming of the day when Sophie could join in. He squeezed his eyes even tighter and imagined what her voice would be like. Higher than his, but smoother, he supposed. Much like the way she was humming at the moment. His imagination took that hum and slowly magnified it until it grew to a full howl.

Aroooooo, he'd sing.

Aroooooo, she would echo.

If he imagined hard enough, he could hear their voices mingle and carry out over the ocean. Their song would join the moonlight, the dancing waves, and the stars, adding a whole new layer of beauty to the scene.

One by one, the dogs trotted over and sat around him and Sophie. Chase didn't stop howling to look, but he could feel them jostle for position and settle down. That came with the occasional grunt and bump, but he ignored all that and continued howling. When a wolf howled, it was with his mind, body, and soul, so it was hard not to get swept up in the sound. So swept up, in fact, that his imagination got more and more carried away. He pictured Sophie's voice joining his, softly at first, then louder. Near and clear enough to seem real.

His eyes snapped open, and his head turned. His howl faded away, but a voice still rang out over the sea.

Sophie's voice. Sophie's howl.

He blinked a few times just to make sure he wasn't dreaming. Had Sophie really shifted into wolf form?

There she sat with her front paws neatly arranged before her lean, canine body and her dainty muzzle aimed upward.

He held his breath. She was the most beautiful wolf he'd ever seen. Her howl was heavenly, with the same soft, clear syllables she made when she spoke. Her coat was the same shiny, chestnut color as her hair — so distinctive, he could have picked her out of a crowd at a glance.

But... but... He sputtered.

But what? Darcy seemed to say. *My nice lady can do anything.*

Sophie held on to her last note then quietly released it, listening to the sound drift away on the wind. Then she opened her eyes, revealing that gorgeous forest green, and looked at him.

Wow. Her murmur registered in his mind. *You're right. That feels so good.* Then she lifted one paw and stared at it. *And, oh my God. Look at me. I'm really a wolf.*

He nodded eagerly. *You are. And you did it by yourself.*

She turned one way then another, looking over her new body. *One minute, I was humming, wishing I could join you, and the next, I was howling. It just happened.* She looked flabbergasted. *It didn't even hurt.*

There was so much he wanted to say and ask and do. But there would be time for all that later. The moon was sinking slowly toward the horizon, and his wolf instincts overrode the impulse to question her. So he lifted his chin slowly, watching to see if Sophie did the same. When she did, he closed his eyes, took a deep breath, and howled again. A howl as happy and proud as he'd ever made

Arooooooo...

Sophie didn't even have to wait a few beats to find her way into the song. Her voice just slipped in alongside his, and together, they sent a serenade up to the stars. Their voices lifted, dropped, and rose again, with her sweet alto an octave above his. Chase's heart pounded as loud and steady as a metronome. And when he really tuned in, he could feel Sophie's heart thumping too. He leaned gently against her side, feeling more grounded than ever before.

One by one, the dogs joined in as well — some more, some less in tune. Even so, it sounded great. Just like the old days in his mother's wolf pack, where everyone would gather around and join in a group howl. One big, happy family, even if they were a scrappy one.

Chase had seen humans go to church, hold hands, and say *Amen.* Howling was a lot like that, in a sense. A celebration of life, love, and values. A time to marvel in the magic of the universe. A way to reinforce mutual bonds.

So he howled his heart out until he grew hoarse. Even then, he went on singing, because he couldn't bear to stop. Sophie sang with all her heart, using instinct to guide her well as they warbled through a duet.

It was beautiful. Perfect. Timeless. Perhaps the best moment of his entire life, even if he knew there was trouble brewing in the shifter world. Moira was still out there, and rumors of the mysterious dragon slayer kept rolling in. Sooner or later, he would have to leave his bubble of newfound bliss and face the outside world again. But for now...

Chase howled away, the happiest wolf there'd ever been. The moon touched the horizon then slid lower until only the upper edge showed as a bright glow. After a deep inhale, he and Sophie howled one more time — a long, low note. They released it the way a child might blow a soap bubble and let it drift away on the wind. Then they leaned against each other and listened as the howl carried across the ocean and faded.

But it didn't disappear so much as it became part of all the other sounds out there.

Magic, Sophie whispered in his mind. *We made magic.*

Chase turned and nuzzled her neck. *Sure did.*

She sighed, sounding sad, but then brightened. *Do we get to do this tomorrow night too?*

He laughed and cuddled closer. *We get to do this forever, my mate.*

Books by Anna Lowe

Aloha Shifters - Pearls of Desire

Rebel Dragon (Book 1)

Rebel Bear (Book 2)

Rebel Lion (Book 3)

Rebel Wolf (Book 4)

Rebel Alpha (Book 5)

Aloha Shifters - Jewels of the Heart

Lure of the Dragon (Book 1)

Lure of the Wolf (Book 2)

Lure of the Bear (Book 3)

Lure of the Tiger (Book 4)

Love of the Dragon (Book 5)

Lure of the Fox (Book 6)

The Wolves of Twin Moon Ranch

Desert Hunt (the Prequel)

Desert Moon (Book 1)

Desert Wolf: Complete Collection (Four short stories)

Desert Blood (Book 2)

Desert Fate (Book 3)

Desert Heart (Book 4)

Desert Yule (a short story)

Desert Rose (Book 5)

Desert Roots (Book 6)

Sasquatch Surprise (a Twin Moon spin-off story)

Blue Moon Saloon

Perfection (a short story prequel)

Damnation (Book 1)

Temptation (Book 2)

Redemption (Book 3)

Salvation (Book 4)

Deception (Book 5)

Celebration (a holiday treat)

Shifters in Vegas

Paranormal romance with a zany twist

Gambling on Trouble

Gambling on Her Dragon

Gambling on Her Bear

Serendipity Adventure Romance

Off the Charts

Uncharted

Entangled

Windswept

Adrift

Travel Romance

Veiled Fantasies

Island Fantasies

visit www.annalowebooks.com

About the Author

USA Today and Amazon bestselling author Anna Lowe loves putting the "hero" back into heroine and letting location ignite a passionate romance. She likes a heroine who is independent, intelligent, and imperfect – a woman who is doing just fine on her own. But give the heroine a good man – not to mention a chance to overcome her own inhibitions – and she'll never turn down the chance for adventure, nor shy away from danger.

Anna loves dogs, sports, and travel – and letting those inspire her fiction. On any given weekend, you might find her hiking in the mountains or hunched over her laptop, working on her latest story. Either way, the day will end with a chunk of dark chocolate and a good read.

Visit AnnaLoweBooks.com

Made in the USA
Columbia, SC
29 August 2021

44538703R00133